THE KING
IN
ACADEMIC GARB

An Autobiography Of HRM Oba Professor Akinola A. Owosekun

THE KING IN ACADEMIC GARB

Paperback ISBN: 978-1-957809-42-7

Hardcover ISBN: 978-1-957809-43-4

Published by:
Cornerstone Publishing
A Division of Cornerstone Creativity Group LLC
Info@thecornerstonepublishers.com
www.thecornerstonepublishers.com

Author's Contact

To book the author to speak at your next event or to order bulk copies of this book, please, send email to:

moroconsult@yahoo.com

Printed in the United States of America.

DEDICATION

This book is dedicated to:

My Economics students at Bowen University, Iwo, Nigeria, who wanted to know how I became who I am, and who want to be like me.

ACKNOWLEDGMENTS

The thought of an autobiography weighed on my mind for a very long time. My intention was to publish it on my seventieth birthday but when that was not realizable, I postponed it to my eightieth. Even with the ten years elongation, I needed constant reminder from my wife who believes very strongly that failure to document my life history would be a missed opportunity to influence so many lives. I thank the Almighty God that this effort has now come to fruition.

I am appreciative of the inspiration I got from my cousin, Mr. Ogunniyi James, who impressed on me the need to document my experience on the throne and the royal family history. In line with this I have provided detailed accounts of the "Epic Battle for Ota-Ide" and the Family Tree of the Owosekun Ruling House.

Mention should also be made of the hundreds of my Economics students at Bowen University, Iwo, Nigeria, who during my eleven years of teaching at Bowen were most curious to know how I became who I am so that they could be like me. I am deeply flattered by their admiration for me and I hope that they will find this autobiography intriguing and inspiring. They should understand now, why I always sermonized that, regardless of their current academic performance, they could still, by determination and hard work, be whatever they wish to be. I have dedicated this autobiography to Bowen University students in the belief that, regardless of current happenings, their generation holds the brightest hope for the future of this country.

I also acknowledge the inspiration and interest of all of those who have previewed this book. They include not only my wife, but also my daughters Morounmubo and Jolaade, who read it more than once because it helped them (explained by their mother) to know their father.

I am grateful to Chief Oyeniyi Akande, the Agba-Akin of Isotun, for accepting to review the book and to prepare the "book review". In like manner, I am grateful to Professor J. A. Faniran, my senior colleague at Bowen University, for accepting to write the foreword to this book.

Additionally, I am very grateful to all those who have in other meaningful ways contributed to the writing and production of this book.

Akinola Adeniyi Owosekun

CONTENTS

FOREWORD

Writing about oneself, in other words, writing an autobiography well is a tortuous task. To present oneself objectively and dispassionately requires extraordinary courage and honesty. It requires a physical and mental distancing of self from self and writing about self in the third person without bias. This is the minimum form of deliberate transposition that will give the autobiographical product the required beneficial lesson to the audience/reader. An autobiography is aimed at telling one's story, first and foremost, for the benefit of the audience/reader. The benefit to the autobiographer is the opportunity to tell the story and convince the reader that the story is worth telling. In other words, it is not a monologue plea to justify what the writer did or did not do or what was done or not done to the writer. It is, therefore, an intricate and even possibly an ultimate philanthropic exercise requiring high presentation skills of selfless empathy because the audience/reader is the *raison d'etre* for the book. Like the proverbial customer, the reader is king. The autobiographer freely educates and guides the readers how he/she navigated life's dark alleys. The proof of a successful autobiography, therefore lies in the extent to which it can serve as a reference book for understanding and solving life's challenges. Although no two life challenges are the same, the categories and genres are near universal.

Having said this little about the presentation and duties of the autobiographer, it remains for us to look at the content and its possible adaptability or applicability. Kabiyesi, Prof Akin Owosekun, presented his story from birth through schools, Colleges, the University, his career and enthronement. He is a product of an ascriptive aristocracy to which he added a prescriptive Western elite aristocracy. The combination which is rare indeed makes his story unique. Very few people share such combination which his father had prophesied many years before it materialized. His story is also unique in the sense that it started at a time that the strong British colonial hands held sway in a unified Nigeria where Kabiyesi, Prof Akin Owosekun was born in Jos. He was born just a few years before the Jos Riot of 1947 but his father earn a seat in the Northern House of Assembly. This was not a mean feat for an Ijesa man of Lagos extraction. Kabiyesi, Prof Akin Owosekun thus has a cosmopolitan background which he stamped with his pupilage at the Baptist Academy, one of the three pillars of secondary education in Nigeria. It was at the 'Bapt Acad' as the school was affectionately called that the young Akin Owosekun struck the favour of two of his teachers, Hal Sheller and Jim Jenson that gave him, his fiancée and his siblings the opportunity of an American education. The lesson here is the value and importance of relationships. At the Comprehensive High School, Aiyetoro, where the author proceeded for the Higher School Certificate Course, he proved his future prospects. He was the best in History and English as well as star athlete and footballer. That earned him appointment as the Athletics Captain and Head of Crimson House. Having won the National John F. Kennedy Essay Competition, he brought the School to limelight. When he did not resume for the second year early because he was sitting the GCE Advanced Level London examination, the School was jittery and offered him a school scholarship as attraction. This is the second take home of the Autobiography that hard work pays because there are people who watch and reward excellence. Those who bring glory to an organization or country richly deserve their rewards. Any system that does not reward excellence or instead rewards mediocrity heads for collapse.

Kabiyesi, Prof Akin Owosekun, paid attention to his siblings and family. Just as he was instrumental in ferrying his fiancée to the U S in search of the golden fleece, he also ensured through adventitious contacts in the U S that his siblings got higher education. It was great and commendable responsibility at a tender age. His sacrifice upgraded the family and thus made each member financially independent. He himself was still pursuing graduate studies at Claremont Graduate School which he completed successfully on August 30, 1973 and returned to Nigeria on September 19, 1973. It is noteworthy that he returned to Nigeria nineteen days after completing his studies in spite of beautiful offers in the United States. This is because at that time Nigeria was still enjoying a golden age. It was a country where life and property were secure. Jobs were available for those qualified and there was security of tenure. It would have been foolhardy to take that kind of decision in the Nigeria of 2022. Talking about the Nigeria of 1973, Dr Owosekun as he was then known took up an appointment as Lecturer at the Ahmadu Bello University, Zaria in 1973. Then Nigeria was a melting pot of ethnic groups while it has become a country of exaggerated ethnic differences and avoidable plurailites. The life of Kabiyesi has seen immeasurable pluralization of the Nigerian society in which every Nigerian longs to move 'home'. Unfortunately, even then there was incipient ethnic tension as some jobs were reserved for people of Northern extraction while Southerners were only hired on contract. It was no surprise then when Dr Owosekun opted to take up the appointment at the Nigerian Institute of Social and Economic Research (NISER), Ibadan.

The NISER tour of duty was not without its challenges which were both institutional and personal. Some were explainable by the perceived professional arrogance of Dr Owosekun while others attributed it to normal individual differences. Be that as it may, it was hurtful to Dr (later Prof) Owosekun in terms of promotion and posting. Fortunately, his expertise

and competence blossomed through several career postings which included the National Planning Commission, the Lagos State Government, United Nations Institute of Development and Planning in Dakar, Senegal, and the Industrial Technical Assistance Project in the Ministry of Industries (ITAP), Abuja. These specialist postings afforded him the opportunity to develop further expertise and more importantly to meet high level technocrats who leveraged his career in the tumultuous waters. The string of specialized postings was followed with appointment with the strategic National Economic Intelligence Committee (NEIC). Unfortunately, NISER, his primary appointment was not happy with this and, for the second time, attempted to terminate his appointment. Actually, cheques were issued for finally disengaging him from NISER. The disengagement was aborted by superior advice and intervention at the highest governmental levels. The plan consumed the arrowhead of planned retirement who was forced to retire. Shortly after, Prof Owosekun was appointed the Director of the Independent Policy Group (IPG), an outfit which had been set up to advise President Olusegun Obasanjo who assumed office in May 1999. Prof Owosekun thus climbed to the highest corridor of power on 18th March 2004. The lesson of Prof Owosekun's career is that challenges and frustrations are not enough to give up on a career. Quitters are failures. The bright light is only at the end of the tunnel. At the very peak of his career, Kabiyesi, Prof Akin Owosekun was not only a King, he advised Kings and the President. He vacated the company of ordinary people, I will not say mean men. Two prophesies came to pass in his life: one by his father and the other by himself. His father had prophesied at a most improbable time that his son would ascend the throne of his ancestors which had been denied to his grandfather. That came to pass when Prof Owosekun ascended the throne in 1988. The second was his prophesy for himself which he rendered at a time he hardly knew what it meant. He had prophesied that he would be Dean of a Faculty in a University. And he became the Dean of the Faculty of Social and Management Sciences in 2015, decades after the prophecy. Kabiyesi, Professor Akin Owosekun has put together his life of promise and fulfilment which was attained by vanquishing trials and tribulations. He once offered his own resignation which was overruled and his appointment was once terminated without due process which also came to nought. Surely, those who are burdened and persecuted in this world of care have a ready model in Prof Akin Owosekun who, in spite of all daunting odds, rose to royalty and academic excellence.

Prof J. A. Faniran, FAS

PREFACE

THE KING IN ACADEMIC GARB: AN AUTOBIOGRAPHY OF HIS ROYAL MAJESTY OBA PROFESSOR AKINOLA A. OWOSEKUN has thirteen chapters, starting with an Introduction which chronicles the history of the traditional rulership in hometown Isotun and how his grandfather, after declining to ascend to the throne of his ancestors, had emigrated to Lagos in order to avoid further pressures and joined the Police Force in 1896. The Introduction concluded with the ascension to the throne by the author in 1988 as Oba Owosekun II, the eighth Asotun of Isotun.

Chapters Two and Three treat his birth and early life in Jos and his primary and secondary education in Lagos and how his future was almost blighted by a decision by his father not to support his further education even though able to do so financially.

In Chapter Four, aptly titled "The Wheel of Fortune," the author narrates how fortune smiled on him through a teacher he had met in his secondary school days who didn't only assist Owosekun to pursue his further education in the United States of America (USA) but also paved the way for his fiancée and his siblings to study in the USA.

Chapter Five is on his return to Nigeria, first to join the Faculty of Social Sciences at Ahmadu Bello University, Zaria and, later, to move to the Nigerian Institute of Social and Economic Research, Ibadan (NISER).

"Existential Threats" and "The Proverbial Nine Lives" are the titles of Chapters Six and Seven which, together, present the rather gory working experiences of Owosekun in NISER and in the Federal Ministry of Industries where he set up a World Bank-sponsored "Industrial Technical Assistance Project" (ITAP), better known in NISER as the "Policy Analysis Department" (PAD). PAD was to prepare for Nigeria a new tariff book, and also to elaborate a number of macroeconomic models on Computable General Equilibrium, System Dynamics, and Input-Output Analysis. It was also to prepare an Industrial Master Plan similar to that adopted then by the Asian Tigers.

These two chapters narrate the very harrowing and frustrating experiences Owosekun went through while honestly, patriotically and very capably discharging those assignments, targeting positive socioeconomic transformation of Nigeria. With the benefit of hindsight, a discerning reader can easily realise that Nigeria was the worse loser when corrupt Nigerian civil servants deliberately killed the project simply because they couldn't get Owosekun to "dip *hands into the [project's] till*" to bribe them as handsomely as they had wished. Yes, the corrupt officials got Owosekun out of the way, but they also thus threw away the baby with the bath water!

Both chapters also show how much shenanigans the World Bank and similar multilateral organisations could often play to undermine the economies of Third World countries in favour of the industrialised Western countries. The author puts it thus: "*Unknown to us, the consulting firm was working under instructions to ensure that the tariff determination favoured the importation of goods not domestic production. This required the statistical manipulation of the estimated tariffs. Until I had this experience, I had always believed that the World Bank was impeccable…evidence [later] provided by the Registrar of Companies in Britain showed that the consulting firm was not even in existence at the time it was awarded the contract by the World Bank*"!

The last part of Chapter Seven deals with the author's meritorious services as the Director of the Independent Policy Group,

President Obasanjo's Policy Think Tank, from 2004 to 2007, and Owosekun's teaching experience at Bowen University, Iwo, for the next eleven years, from September 2007. Those two posts provided a contrasting respite to his previous turbulent public service experiences—so much so that, perhaps, he could have better given them a separate chapter, under the possible title of "Life after NISER".

Chapter Eight, titled "Beware What You Wish for Yourself", opens with a prophetic boast by the author's father that, if he did not himself become a king, at least one of his sons would. It narrates how Owosekun (until then known as Akinola JAMES) retraced his family tree back to Isotun and visited the place for the first time in 1964 on a mere adventure of curiosity only to, by Providence, become its king in 1988. The chapter also details his struggles and successes in retrieving for the stool of Asotun its rights as a first-class oba and to wear the culturally much-coveted beaded crown.

Chapter Nine, "Epic Battle Over Ota-Ide", takes the reader through the labyrinth of Yoruba customary land tenure system and the author's very successful efforts, though protracted and full of melodrama, at reclaiming for his domain some farmsteads earlier furtively appropriated by tenants on Isotun's land. The chapter gives also an insight into intrigues in Ijesa traditional politics.

Chapter Ten, "Development Experience", summarises the socioeconomic advancements which Isotun and its environs had witnessed since 1988, courtesy of Oba Owosekun II, who used his personal resources and political connections and influences to improve infrastructures in education, healthcare delivery, water supply, transportation and electricity to communities which had, before his ascension, suffered abysmal neglect by governments at all levels. As an icing on the cake, he was instrumental to the granting of a piece of land for the establishment of a private university there.

Chapter Eleven, "Paradise Lost and Paradise Regained", reveals how his revulsion at the racism he saw in a black community in America had forced the author to query "*whether there was one God for the whites and another for the blacks*" or where's the fairness of God if He was "*so kind to one race and so much more less compassionate to another*"?

Though he had been born into a Christian home, attended churches where he had played roles as membership of choirs and a Sunday School teacher and attended Christian mission schools all his life back in Nigeria prior to the experience in the USA, he went through a religious crisis for a 20-year period when he became agnostic. However, he eventually returned to his Christian faith and has, since 1986, not only become a regular churchgoer but also held very important key church leadership positions and has given financial support to many philanthropic causes.

Chapter Twelve is a summary on the biographical sketches of members of the author's nuclear family.

The book concludes with Chapter 13, THE EVENTIDE. The chapter dwells on the author's activities post-retirement from the Nigerian civil/public service, undertakings which he originally conceived for generating, by his bootstrap, incomes necessary to enable him maintain as much as possible the standard of living he had been accustomed to while holding public offices. The chapter recounts some of such activities for which he used his private limited liability consultancy company to execute between 2006 and 2022; the chapter concludes that they were not only financially rewarding but professionally satisfying to the author.

The assignments executed included helping the National Planning Commission to design, elaborate and develop programmes for generating double digit Gross Domestic Product growth rate consistently for a period of 10 to 15 years; for raising Nigeria's per capita income so much that Nigeria could become a member of the elite club of the Upper-Middle Income Developing Countries by 2050; and for generating high level of employment, thus reducing the incidence of poverty in Nigeria to less than 10 million people by 2050.

The autobiography of HRM Oba Professor Akinola A. Owosekun – Oba Owosekun II, for short – is a fascinating guide, through his unique perspective, of the history of Nigeria from the end of the colonial era to the early hopeful days of independence to our current national situation. It takes the reader through all the ups and downs of our national story. It is a good introduction to the history of Nigeria for a reader without any prior context of Nigeria. Even for those of us who have gone through a similar journey, Oba Owosekun's perspective awakens our nostalgia and brings back to mind many memories of the forks along our path as a nation and it chronicles clearly how we arrived at the current situation we find ourselves in.

Oba Owosekun's history is fascinating because, as he himself readily admits, it would have been impossible for any logical person to predict his path from a child born in colonial Nigeria to a father who, though himself well educated and financially able, suddenly became disinterested in supporting his son's education and to a mother who could not afford to pay for his education to becoming a professor of economics who worked with Governor Lateef Jakande of Lagos State on designing and monitoring the 1981-1985 Economic Development Plan, which is widely recognized as the golden period of Lagos's development; to becoming an integral part of the team that built the 1989 Industrial Master Plan for the government of

General Ibrahim Gbadamosi Babangida; and the man who worked as the head of the Independent Policy Group (IPG), the policy think tank for the second term of President Olusegun Obasanjo from 2004 till 2007.

Apart from recording his varied and numerous professional achievements, Oba Owosekun's book serves as an excellent memoir on navigating the labyrinth of the Nigerian civil service from independence, its early promises and how it quickly ran aground on the quicksand of personal ambitions, corruption, nepotism and lack of a clear direction from ever-changing administrations. His path through the various agencies created to fast-track Nigeria's economic revolution is a sorry tale of how we lost our way as a nation and how all the excellent research and works done by dedicated people in the system were largely allowed to go to waste.

It is rare to see someone reach the height of their careers in different areas of life, but the author is both a professor and a Yoruba first class Oba. The autobiography tells the story of how a boy born in Jos to a father surnamed "James", traced back his roots to the historical town of Isotun and rediscovered his ancestral roots and surname of "Owosekun" to which he quickly reverted in 1964. The book recounts the stranger-than-fiction story of how he was made – against his own original desires – to ascend the throne of his fathers, purely on his own terms. It tells the story of his leadership of the town of Isotun in the last 35 or so years and gives the reader hope that a people can make quick and tremendous progress in their development provided that they have a selfless and patriotic leader like Oba Owosekun.

The question any reasonable person is probably asking, then, is how did Oba Owosekun achieve so much in his first 80 years of life so far? The author himself, looking back over his life, has this to say in the book: *I carefully reviewed… my entire life. It was a life full of favor and mercy from "Some Being". It could not have been an accident… so, who was this Being that took so much interest in my affairs? After a long period of examination…, I concluded that the Almighty God was that "Being".*

He gives all the credit for his life to the unsearchable and underserved grace of God. However, many of us will know and agree that the grace of God in human affairs works through means, and we find plenty of those means in this book. The importance of kind people who took interest in Oba Owosekun throughout his life up to date cannot be overstated. His American teacher at Baptist Academy, Lagos– Hal Sheller – who became the force behind his education in the US and whose family history, across three generations, has remained intertwined with that of the Owosekuns is a prominent example. There were also many other numerous helpers throughout his academic and professional careers, coming from the most unlikely sources. For example, the author has this to say: *when as we shall see later, my professional career experienced an existential threat, my northern professional colleagues/friends were more helpful, reliable, and faithful than most of the professional colleagues/friends of my own ethnic group.*

Another means used by God for the advancement of Oba Owosekun is his intimidating intelligence. The book doesn't say much on this simply because the author is too reserved to blow his own trumpet loudly, but any discerning reader, reading between the lines, would be able to see how at every stage in his career, he stood heads and shoulders above his contemporaries in mental capacity and how every task or assignment given to him was always delivered beyond the expectations of his teachers and superiors.

However, the intelligence of the author should not be taken as the only or even the major factor that accounts for his rise. Oba Owosekun is clearly someone who learnt a lifelong lesson on the importance of hard work and determination based on a traumatic experience in his early life. As he says: *I was in primary*

four and in the first term of that school year I was in the 47th position in a class of fifty (50). My brothers and sister performed much better. My parents were no longer around. I remained one of the best dressed, with beautiful creep sandals and glittering rain boots but I was a dunce. The humiliation of this failure more than the denial of privileges by our guardian, was so unbearable that I made an irrevocable life resolution of "NEVER AGAIN". The resolution was a game changer such that in the last term of the year, I was 4th, and the worst position I held throughout the rest of primary school was 3rd.

This life resolution to always put in his best effort is clearly something that has never left him from that period, and which showed in his dedication to every project he carried out.

Anybody reading this review thus far would assume that Oba Owosekun's life has been an easy one. That assumption could not be farther from the truth. His life seems to be a living illustration of Tai Solarin's dictum: *'May Your Road Be Rough'*. Oba Owosekun's road has certainly been rough. From persecutions throughout his career; to legal and diabolic battles from well-placed opponents as an Oba trying to serve his community; to losing his only son who had struggled with persistent illness throughout his life, the author understands adversity well. But as Solarin also said: *Life, if it is going to be abundant, must have plenty of hills and vales. It must have plenty of sunshine and rough weather. It must be packed with days of danger and of apprehension.*

Oba Owosekun certainly has a reason for why he has chosen Psalms 23 and 91 as his favourite biblical passages as they describe the journey of a man who has walked through the valley of the shadow of death, but who through the grace of God has been able to overcome every adversity and ascend to the mountaintop.

Perhaps this history of adversity and self-reflection explains why the author is so candid about his own flaws. This is not

a whitewashed story like many of the autobiographies of many prominent people where they are always right and their enemies always wrong. For example, Oba Owosekun, reflecting on a dispute he had during a job interview, has this to say about his own personality: *Nevertheless, one of my most nauseating professional weaknesses--snobbishness--which I must have inculcated at Claremont, was beginning to clearly manifest.* A wise reader would learn from such self-honesty for, as Aristotle put it, *"knowing yourself is the beginning of all wisdom"*.

The author has dedicated this very insightful autobiography to his students at Bowen University, Iwo who had frequently asked him how he became what he was then as their teacher and they expressed willingness to be like him. However, could it be that Owosekun had not himself observed or that his modesty has not allowed him to admit that even his colleagues, his staff and associates with whom he has worked and closely interacted over time, too, might be silently wondering how he has become the enigma he is? Perhaps many of them may privately want to be like him! Otherwise, how does one explain the ease with which Owosekun was able to reassemble in Chapter 13 the very highly professional and experienced people with whom his consultancy firm executed the various projects he secured after their respective retirements, most of them old hands?

Very apposite in this context is the example of a director in the National Planning Commission who invited Owosekun in 2019 to carry out a training programme on the elaboration of macroeconomic models and input-output analysis and who thus paved the way for other very challenging projects. Owosekun described that director as having "been my Research Assistant in virtually every Ministry, Department and Agency (MDA) in which I had served" before retirement. To carry out the assignments, the author shrewdly "put together a team comprising very experienced professionals...[which] included my longtime associate and colleague...since 1982". To retain such a cult-like loyalty from both staff and professional colleagues speaks eloquently to Owosekun's high capacity for excellent human relations and management and loyalty to his friends.

A few threads run through the autobiography but they are clearly highlighted by the assignments carried out by the author and his company during the twilight of his professional contributions to the country's socioeconomic development reported on in Chapter 13. They reflect clearly some of his personality traits especially: his being able to identify and nurture good staff; his ability to keep friends over a long time; his being highly regarded by people he has ever worked with at all levels; his maintaining a very high mental alertness and an unusually strong perspicacity of mind; his uncanny organisational skills; his incredible stamina for very rigorous thinking; and his indefatigable determination to carry through any assignment--even at close to 80 years of age...!

In Chapter 7, the autobiography shows how some powerful staffers of the National Planning Commission had, for their selfish corrupt reasons, killed a department which Owosekun had ably established for the improvement of Nigeria's macroeconomic planning processes. It is gratifying that the last chapter of his autobiography, Chapter 13, concludes on the happy note that the same National Planning Commission invited the very same Owosekun to "reinvent the same processes" with applause. Yes, as the author himself admits, it's difficult to conclude if those high hopes for Nigeria envisaged in the projects recounted in Chapter 13 would be realised or not. Yet, one really rejoices with Owosekun, the proverbial rejected stone which became the main pillar of the building.

And one celebrates his accomplishments due largely to his tenacity of purpose as one reechoes Owosekun's very deep final sentence in this final chapter of the autobiography:

"Who would have thought that these contributions to knowledge and the development efforts reported in this chapter would be realisable in the twilight of my mortality".

I therefore have no hesitation in commending this short but punchy autobiography to the reading public. Reading it will not only be a literary pleasure but would also allow the reader to learn from a veritable national treasure. It is no wonder that his students at Bowen University wanted to know how he became who he is and wanted to become more like him. After reading this book, you too will have learnt something from him and would wish that the book had not ended so quickly!

Oyeniyi AKANDE

CHAPTER 1

INTRODUCTION

According to the history of the Ijesas, Ajibogun Ajaka, Owa Obokun Onida Arara, who was acclaimed as the most accomplished son of Oduduwa succeeded his father as the Olofin, and was the first ruler over Ijesaland. He was succeeded by Owaka Okile, and by a string of other Princes as Owa of Ijesaland. These other princes included Owa Obokun Billagbayo, 1713 to 1733, after whom one of the four Ruling Houses in Ijesaland is named. Owa Billagbayo was succeeded by his son, Owa Billajagodo Arijelesin, 1749 to 1771, whose descendants included Owa Ataiyero Bi Agogo, 1902 to 1920, and Atari-Agbo (Obuko o l'ori ati ba Agbo kan) who was the first Asotun of Isotun, 1823 to 1852. Atari-Agbo was a warrior and his domain of Isotun was located on the boundary of Ijesaland and Ede, demarcated by the Shasha River. The Ijesas sometimes refer to the Ijesa/Ede boundary as Ota-ide. Atari-Agbo was famously charged with checking the incursion of the Timi of Ede into Ijesaland.

Atari-Agbo had only two surviving sons namely, Gbatoremu and Adegboro Owosekun. They both succeeded their father, in turns as Asotun of Isotun, 1852 to 1874 and 1874 to 1916, respectively. The son of Gbatoremu, Igbalajobi, went on to become the Aloya of Iloya while one of the sons of Adegboro

Owosekun, Ayeni Ale, declined contesting the Owaship during the 1894-1896 vacancy. In order to avoid further pressure on him to contest the Owaship he migrated to Lagos where he joined the Lagos Police Force which was established in 1896. While in Lagos, Ayeni Ale, converted to Christianity and was baptized at the First Baptist Church on Broad Street in 1899. He took the Christian name "James" which he made his children bear as their last name. On April 1st, 1913 Ayeni Ale was blessed with a son, Solomon Oke James, as his third child. Solomon Oke James spent most of his adult life in Bukuru/Jos, now in Plateau State, and served as a Special Member of the Northern House of Assembly terminating in 1957, following which he relocated to Lagos. Honourable Solomon Oke James, married Cecilia Bolaji James (nee Suberu) in 1942, and was the father of HRM Oba Professor Akinola Adeniyi Owosekun, Owosekun II, who was installed the eighth Asotun of Isotun on 9th April 1988.

Owu-Ipole which was reported to have been founded in the 9th or 10th century AD, is currently referred to as Orile Owu. Yoruba history acknowledges Orile Owu as the second Yoruba settlement to be founded after Ile-Ife. However, in the 1800's there was a mutual dislike by both communities for each other largely because Ile-Ife disparaged Orile Owu for its treatment of refugees from the Old Oyo Empire. Orile Owu was accused of subjecting these refugees to forced labour and slavery.

In 1821, this mutual dislike between the two settlements degenerated into armed conflict following which Apomu, a major slave trading market near Ikire, which was under the direct control of Ile-Ife, was overrun by Orile Owu. The Owus secured Apomu by installing one of their own as the traditional ruler. Ile-Ife then solicited the help of several Yoruba settlements and was obliged by many of them including Ijebu and Ikoyi. In 1828, Ile-Ife and its allies prevailed over Orile Owu. Thus, the Orile-Owu-installed traditional ruler of Apomu, was sacked. Orile Owu itself was in ruins.

One of the four children of the Orile-Owu-installed traditional ruler of Apomu was Olayinka whose four children were: Adewoyun, Orisagbeolu (Obasa), a daughter who was later addressed as "Iya Idumota", and Suberu Olaleye. The first two, Adewoyun and Orisagbeolu, resettled in Abeokuta in "Adewoyun's Compound", Oke-Saje. Some of their prominent descendants included the late Alhaji Lateef Adewoyun who was the Otun of Apomu-Owu, Abeokuta, and the late Alhaji Raheem Bello who was the Imam of Oke-Saje. The daughter (Iya Idumota) and her brother, Suberu Olaleye resettled in Lagos where "Iya Idumota" later became the "Olori Agba" of Oba Esugbayi, the Eleko of Eko, 1901-1925 and 1931-1932.

Historical records show that Oba Esugbayi was the grandson of Oba Dosunmu the First. He was deposed by the Colonial Masters in 1925 for his failure to dissociate himself from the Privy Council Address of Herbert Macaulay in respect of the "Oluwa land case." Oba Esugbayi was accused of insisting on the Title of Eleko of Eko and of refusing among other things to adopt, as the Colonial Masters demanded, a denunciation of Herbert Macaulay's address at the Privy Council. The denunciation was drafted by the famous educator and administrator, Henry Rawlingson Carr.

However, following the determination of his appeal by the Privy Council in 1931, Oba Esugbayi was re-instated. In the period of his dethronement, Oba Ibikunle Akintoye reigned from 1925 to 1928 and Oba Sanusi Olusi reigned from 1928 to 1931, when he stepped down for the re-instatement of Oba Esugbayi.

3

The fourth child, Suberu Olaleye, was highly indulged by the "Olori Agba" who obliged him to reside at "Oko Olori". He was later to earn the Islamic Title of "Seriki Musilumi" at the first Central Mosque, Ebute Metta. Suberu Olaleye had fifty children amongst whom was Momoh, the father of Mrs. Cecilia Bolaji who was my mother. Cecilia Bolaji James (nee Suberu) was therefore a Princess in her own right.

Parentage

Deaconess. Cecilia Bolaji
James, My Mom

Hon. Solomon Oke James,
My Dad

Maternal Uncle (L) and Paternal Uncle with my Dad

CHAPTER 2

EARLY CHILHOOD

I was born on Wednesday, 17th March, 1943, in Jos, now in Plateau State. Beyond this record of event, it is difficult to establish when one begins to remember. Some of those who have gone through this path of writing their respective autobiographies put the age at which one begins to remember at "three". In my case, I will go by my earliest memories prominent among which are the following:

a) I remember that while we were still living in an official residence adjoining the Nigerian Electricity Supply Corporation (NESCO) in Bukuru, a tray of black-eyed beans was placed to dry in the sun in order to force the weevils which had infested the beans to self-evacuate. I reached out to the tray and while playing with the beans I slipped one into my nostril. My efforts to remove it were unsuccessful and by the time I raised an alarm, the bean had swollen because it had absorbed a lot of the moisture in my nose. I ended up in the "hospital" where I woke up with a medical personnel, possibly the doctor, standing by my stretcher (not bed).

b) In the general neighbourhood of our home, there was a branch of a foreign retail store, Gottschalk, whose manager took interest in me and would entice me with candy/sweet anytime

I drove my bicycle wheel in the vicinity of the store. It was the period when Indian mysticism and talisman were in vogue. This manager would entice me into a secured room or keep me right below the canter he was supervising, and then try out his acquired charms on me. He would pronounce some incantations on an awkwardly shaped object (obviously a talisman) and ask whether I saw a genie or some such demon, actualize. I would answer in the negative because in truth I saw nothing. However, after repeated questioning, I would answer in the affirmative to please him and to ensure I did not miss my ration of candy. In much later years when I was in primary VI, I was to have another experience with Indian talisman and charms. Indeed, at that time catalogues of these charms describing their efficacy and how to order for them were published and widely circulated. There were in our class, a few grown-ups such as Emmanuel, Samson and William who were much older than the rest of us and were already dating or were anxious to start dating. We now lived in Surulere, in an area where the wells were shallow and toads/frogs were commonly found. I was approached one day by William to help him with a toad. William lived in Alago-meji at Adekunle bus-stop, and had developed interest in the use of Indian charms to cultivate amorous relationships with girls. He owned a catalogue and was particularly interested in the magical handkerchief, the facial powder and a particular ring. He explained that if you robbed the handkerchief on your face or applied the powder on the face, the targeted female would fall prey instantly on looking at your face. He was approaching me because he had a problem with activating the efficacy of the ring. The ring must first be inserted into the bowel of a toad and buried for several days. Then if you wore it and touched a lady, that lady would instantly become your "slave." I was fascinated by his story and provided whatever help I could. He was in competition with two of his colleagues for Yewande, Tinu and Esther. The last girl was his main target. The adventure turned out to be a mere fantasy, a complete failure. These failed efforts appear to have strongly influenced my scepticism, in much later years, about the efficacy of demonic forces.

c) My parents were guardians to quite a number of their nephews and nieces. I remember that at one point in time there were at least seven of them. As my mother was a seamstress, there were a few other girls on day trips, to learn the trade. I unwittingly became what was then referred to as "The Messenger of Peace" between the girls and their boyfriends who did not have the liberty to freely visit them. I responded to the whistle blowing indicating arrival; carried oral and sometimes written messages to suitors and was amply rewarded by all.

d) Every child of school age in the family attended St. Peter's Anglican School, Bukuru. I did not like attending school and would come up with all kinds of conceivable excuses. I could not be persuaded to go to school except there was the assurance of being taken there in my father's official pickup, or on his messenger's bicycle or on the shoulder of any of my much older cousins. I had so much latitude deciding whether or not to attend school that any day a chicken was to be slaughtered and I was privy to it, I would choose not to go to school. I needed to be home on such occasions to witness the event and to ensure that the prized parts were reserved for me! Needless to say that my academic performance was dismal. I was deeply intrigued much later in life when in my American History Class I read that during the Presidential election of the late 1920's in that country, the campaign slogan of one of the candidates was " a car in every garage and a chicken in every pot."

As a child, I remember living a very comfortable life. From the early 1940's, there was running water and electricity and by 1952, when we moved to a new residence at the sub-station in Bukuru, we had access to a telephone, a modern bath tub with electric heater, a modern toilet with W/C and an electric

9

cooker for the kitchen. I wore a pair of sandals to school on regular days and a pair of fanciful rain-boots on rainy days. I was so thoroughly indulged by my parents that it was generally believed and said that there was no way I would be an achiever in life. On my coronation as the Asotun of Isotun, at least two of those who had held such belief approached me and openly acknowledged how grossly in error they had been. However, I knew deep down in my heart that, but for a shock treatment divinely ordained in my early childhood, I would not have been who I am.

e) In my childhood days it was not fashionable for homes to make provisions for orchards. Fruits were obtainable in the markets or in the wild. The latter was a more veritable source for fresh fruits, and was a lot more fun for children especially. However, in the wild, one must contend with the possibility of encountering monkeys and baboons. Indeed, monkeys and baboons were a common sight, in those days, driving between Barikin Ladi and Kura Falls.

The Nigerian Electricity Supply Company (NESCO) for which my father worked had its major dam in Kura Falls which was a considerable distance from Bukuru, Jos. My father maintained an official residence there and I was always delighted to join him especially during the holidays. On one of such occasions, I was accompanied by our house help and chaperone, Musa, to go on an expedition to the wild for mangoes. In this forest, there was a mango tree which was at the very edge of a tributary of the dam, such that a lot of its branches stretched over the tributary. The Company's notice at the mouth of the tributary drew particular attention to the considerable depth of the dam at that point.

The attraction of this mango tree for me, was that it had a particularly unique specie of mangoes and those mangoes were sufficiently ripe. I chose to reach one of those at the top of the tree but as I stretched out to reach my choice mango, the stump on which I rested my weight broke and I was destined to fall into the tributary. I rapidly began to fall from the tree, toward the water, with my arms outstretched above my head. Miraculously, however, I found my hands latched onto the very last branch of the tree with my feet dangling over the water below. I climbed onto this branch and slowly worked my way back to the trunk, and to safety. Musa. my chaperone, and I were petrified. We took a look at one another and decided unequivocally to return home.

CHAPTER 3

VICISSITUDES IN EARLY LIFE

During my dad's annual leave in late 1953, he started planning to relocate to Lagos after his tenure in the Northern House of Assembly. He commenced the construction of his personal house at Surulere, completing the ground floor by the end of 1954 with the assistance of his brother Mr. 'Sanya James who played a supervisory role. This assistance earned his brother free accommodation in the building for over two decades.

We, the children, were the first to be relocated. In January 1955, four of the children: my senior brother (Olatunbosun) who was a product of my mother's first marriage, junior sister (Bolade), my junior brother (Adewunmi), and I were transferred to Surulere Baptist School on Ojuelegba Road, Surulere. Our uncle was to be our guardian.

This arrangement was not workable, requiring that our mother join us in early 1956 to relieve my uncle of his guardianship. My uncle required us to fetch/buy firewood at Ikate and Ijesa areas which were some two miles from home, for domestic use. Our out-of-pocket allowances were denied us, sometimes in part and at other times in full. The feeding was so bad, we were malnourished. Verbal insults were also frequently hauled at our mother especially.

Horrible though it was, it became the turning point of my life. Given the benefit of hindsight, it was this shock treatment I needed. My performance in school had continued to be dismal. I was in primary four and in the first term of that school year, I was in the 47th position in a class of fifty (50). My brothers and sister performed much better. My parents were no longer around. I remained one of the best dressed, with beautiful creep sandals and glittering rain booths but I was a dunce. The humiliation of this failure more than the denial of privileges by our guardian, was so unbearable that I made an irrevocable life resolution of "NEVER AGAIN." The resolution was a game changer such that in the last term of the year, I was 4th, and the worst position I held throughout the rest of primary school was 3rd. I was beginning to win prizes from primary V!!!

Transition to secondary school was, however, somewhat problematic. I was at the head of my class and should not have had any problem passing the entrance examination to any secondary school of my choice. But instead of following the advice of my Headmaster to choose the Baptist Academy where I was sure to have preferential consideration, I chose the CMS Grammar School whose cut-off, in spite of my near excellent record and confidence, I failed to meet. I was humbled as my father, through his friend, arranged for me to attend mediocre Lagos City College where, because of my distaste for the College, I became a truant, and subsequently approached my primary school for the opportunity to once again attempt the entrance examination to the Baptist Academy. After some hesitation I was allowed to. At the Baptist Academy I made heroic effort to regain lost time and ground. My classmates in Surulere Baptist School who had gained admission in the previous year were now a year my senior. I was lucky to meet in form one, a very ambitious student who was like me--very much in a hurry!!! My English teacher in form one was very proud of my writing skill. At least once, she proudly read my class essay to the graduating class as an example of the standard they should seek to attain.

My friend, Layi Lawson, who was from Holy Cross Primary School on Lagos Island and I, decided to register to take the London General Certificate of Education (GCE) Qualifying Examination in January of the year preceding our resumption in form two (2). We indeed took the examination and to the consternation of our colleagues, we passed. While we were in form three, we sat for the full GCE Examination in the January preceding our resumption in form four (4) and we passed the required five (5) subjects including English. Everyone in school was now fully convinced that our academic performance was not a fluke. Now that we had achieved the ultimate that one could in high school, we were left with what next to do. We decided to stay in school for a while and contemplate the future. However, in November of that year, just as our immediate seniors were about to commence the West African School Certificate Examination, the school appointed me the Acting Senior Prefect, and my friend the Acting Assistant Senior Prefect, to replace the outgoing substantive Senior and Assistant Senior Prefects. So, we decided to remain in school for one more year to fully enjoy the honour bestowed on us. Layi aimed at taking his Advance GCE Examination the January after the completion of our stay at the Baptist Academy and I decided to take mine a year later.

In view of a development in the family, I was beginning to adjust my earlier plan for my future. As a way of encouraging me to be serious with my studies, my father assured me in 1955, after I made my remarkable turnaround at Surulere Baptist School

15

that, if I wished to study on the moon, he was ready to provide the support. Alas! When in 1963 I intimated him of my plan to attend a Higher High School and to earn a university degree, his response was that a high school education was sufficient. Even when my Principal, Dr. J. A. Adegbite, of blessed memory, invited him for a discussion on the subject matter, he did not honour the invitation. He was palpably unyielding. I am minded to think that at least two factors strongly influenced my father's change of heart:

a)   Arguing that it was an abomination for a man in our culture to have children from one wife, my aunt, Ibijoke James, arranged for and forced another wife on my dad.

b)   My father was beginning to have a problem with alcohol and was beginning to keep bad company. On one occasion he raised the issue of my educational ambition with one of his drinking partners, one Mr. Bajulaiye, who was then resident in Bariga, Lagos. This friend made the remark to my hearing that secondary school education was indeed sufficient.

These factors made indelible marks on my lifestyle. They are largely responsible for my cautious abstinence from alcohol and womanizing. But for the fact that my life was divinely driven, my academic career, brilliant as it has been, would have terminated at the secondary school level.

Primary and Secondary Education

At Surulere Baptist School 1957

With Layi Lawson (L) and Chucks Lawrence at the Baptist Academy

CHAPTER 4

THE WHEEL OF FORTUNE

Nevertheless, I successively transited to the higher high school level. Four people in varying degrees made this possible. They were two of my American teachers at the Baptist Academy, Hal Sheller and Jim Jenson, my senior brother, Olatunbosun Ayinde, and my mother. I first gained admission into Olivet Baptist Boys' High School, Oyo, but while plans were being made by Hal Sheller to pay the non-refundable deposit, I received the very same morning, an invitation to attend the interview for the Comprehensive High School Aiyetoro (CHSA) which was my preference. The payment plan to Olivet was aborted while I pursued the admission into CHSA.

At CHSA, I recorded a number of achievements. I was appointed the athletics captain, then the Head of Crimson House. I was the school's major striker on the football team and I won the prestigious John F. Kennedy Memorial Essay Competition. Success at the essay competition earned my school tremendous fame and honour. The school received donation of several books from the American Embassy. Dr. Horace G. Dawson, the Head of the United States Information Service (USIS) in Nigeria, led the United States delegation that made the presentation to the school. I received a certification too.

However, on my admission to CHSA, I assessed my financial situation to be adequate for only one of the two years of study if my father remained adamant. I brought up the matter with my senior brother and we agreed that I should take the Advanced London GCE certificate examination in January of the year preceding my second year at CHSA. I was then, if I passed the examination, to apply for university admission and a university scholarship. My senior brother paid for the advanced London GCE examination the very day the application for the examination was to close.

I resumed late in school in January because I was busy taking the examination. This lateness had caused some concern in school about my inability to continue because of my financial constraint. The concern stemmed from a number of my records. I was the best student in History and in English. In addition, I was a prominent member of the athletics and football teams. My history teacher, Mr. Van Seasholes, was the first teacher I encountered on my resumption. He expressed concern about my lateness and intimated to me that the school management had decided that I be recalled with an offer of a half scholarship. I was appreciative and elated. Next, only some few yards away, between the Library and the Administrative block, I was beaconed by the Vice Principal, Mr. L. A. Sofenwa, who expressed the same concern about my lateness to school and intimated to me the school's decision to offer me a half scholarship and that if it was not sufficient to cover my needs, it would be made full! I was flattered.

In March, the result of the advanced level London GCE was published and I passed in the two subjects History and Economics I had sat for. I immediately applied for admission to the University of Ibadan (UI) and the University of Ife (now Obafemi Awolowo University) to read History which I had developed a great flair for from studying American and Russian

History at CHSA. I was admitted into UI and I resumed 25th September,1965. However, between the time that the advanced level GCE result was announced and the time I resumed at UI, two very important events took place: The first was a visit to me in Aiyetoro by Hal Sheller who, on hearing of my success at the advanced London GCE examination and admission to UI, offered me sponsorship to study in the United States of America. Not fully knowing his background, I confided in him my fear of being stranded in the USA. He assured me that I would not be stranded and immediately asked for pen and paper on which he provided me with the address of the University to which I should apply for admission. After consultation that evening with my longtime friend, Layi Lawson, and my House Master, Mr. M. A. Makinde, I decided to take the offer.

Second, was the result of the John F. Kennedy Memorial Essay competition. The result was announced after I had left CHSA to prepare to resume at UI and/or travel to the United States. I was actually not in school when the American delegation visited. I read of my success in the Memorial Essay Competition in the newspaper: the "Daily Express" while I was on the queue at the Doctor's clinic to complete the medical test required to obtain my international passport. I visited the school at my earliest convenience and was briefed of the need to contact the USIS Office to obtain my certification. At the USIS, I was received by Mrs. Sodeinde who inquired to know why I was not in school at the time of their visit. She was also curious to know my future plans. I intimated to her my admission into UI and that I was now applying for scholarship to finance my education there. She was excited and replied "I will find you one."

Plans for my trip to the US were concluded in November 1965 by Mr. Springwater who was then the Head of the Africa American Institute in Lagos. I visited Mrs. Sodeinde on

7th January, 1966, to brief her of developments and she wished me well. At the University of Ibadan, my History Lecturer was the highly reputed Dr. (Later Professor) Ade Ajayi. He was also my tutorial lecturer which tutorial sessions were held in his office. My lecturer in Economics was the renowned Dr. (Later Professor) Ojetunji Aboyade and my tutorial lecturer was Mr. (later Professor) Bambri. My history class was about the Jihad and Usuman Danfodio. It was not quite as challenging as the American and Russian history I studied at CHSA. I made enquiries about changing my major to Economics and obtained the approval of the Head of the Department of Economics to do so. However, the desk officer for effecting the change in the Registry spoke very eloquently against it. He advised that if I really wanted to study economics I should do so in the United States because, according to him, the study at Ibadan was grossly lacking in quantitative analysis. I was somewhat disappointed but since I had already gained admission to study economics in the United States, I concluded that my effort to change my major to Economics in UI was indeed needless. I returned to the Head of Department who was of European extraction, and who was already expecting to receive/authorize my paper for processing, to inform him that I had aborted the idea without giving him a reason. He looked down to the book that he was reading then raised his head up again and nodded without uttering a word.

Even after I had decided to take the option of studying in the United States, I still had some basic concerns. First, I had confided in Hal Sheller that I did not want to be stranded in the United States. This concern arose largely from my knowledge of American History and the level of poverty, especially among blacks. The Watts riot of 1964 was particularly very revealing of the degree of racism in America. My earlier fears were then rekindled by the arrangement to first attend a Community College which essentially was the first two years of a University. I would be attending College --a two-year college for that matter--then I would transit to a four-year College to complete the last two years to obtain a bachelor's degree. I was leaving the Premier University in Nigeria for a college!

My concern about being stranded was aggravated by the fact that I was to travel by boat on a twenty-day journey from Lagos. These feelings were deep and private and there was no one to confide in. However, I made a number of observations: my future in the University of Ibadan was itself uncertain because the source of funding had dried up. No scholarship had been awarded and Hal Sheller and Jim Jenson had departed from Nigeria. My dad who could have filled the gap by providing the financial resource remained unimpressed.

Incidentally, I observed on one of the documents for my admission to Fullerton Junior College (later named Fullerton College) that one Harry Lynn Sheller was the President of the College. Upon enquiries, Harry Lynn Sheller turned out to be father of Hal Sheller and was actually my sponsor! On the quality standard of the College, I was strongly persuaded that Mr. Springwater of the African American Institute who was responsible for the institutionalised scholarship programme between Nigeria and the United States of America would not have been entrusted with my welfare, visa application and travel arrangements if the offer was fraudulent or demeaning in any way.

I departed Lagos on 14th January, 1966 -- a day before the military coup in Nigeria. The expected 20-day journey by ship took 43 days because of extenuating circumstances at sea. The captain of the cargo ship which had some facilities for passengers, S. S. Fairwind, added some other stops, other than those initially scheduled, to his itinerary. We arrived in Port Harcourt where I learnt of an army mutiny on the 15th of January, 1966. We departed Port Harcourt on the 17th for Abidjan, Côte D'voire, arriving there on the 19th, and on the second day I visited the Abidjan township. Arrival in Matadi was on the 26th. This was emotional for me remembering the Sir Henry Norton Stanley, the British American Explorer, "Bula Matadi". I undertook a tour of the town the following day in the company of a Congolese friend who spoke only French. Next on our itinerary was Lobito in Angola. We arrived there on the 1st of February and stayed till the 4th. I took a tour of Lobito several times but was closely monitored by security agents each time. We arrived in Luanda the following day but I, in person, was denied entry because of my nationality. Thereafter, the trip to the United States was straight forward. We travelled direct to Freetown where Alfred, my sailor friend on the boat, invited me to his house in Freetown for lunch of fufu. We left the same day on an 11-day nonstop trip to the United States. I was documented at Panama City in Florida, United States on the 24th of February, and arrived Houston, Texas, on the 26th for a bus ride to Fullerton, California through Los Angeles.

I lived with the President of my College in their three-bedroom house which had only one bathroom. Needless to say, we all used the same toilet and had our bath in the same bathroom at a time when it was illegal in many States of the Union for blacks to use the same toilets with whites.

I spent one and a half years to finish at Fullerton College. I also made a number of landmark achievements there. I won a position at the Eastern Regional Conference Debate held in Los Angeles, California only a month or so after my enrolment.

I was also President of the International Students Union in which capacity I had a radio conversation with Senator Robert F. Kennedy who was brother to the famed President John F. Kennedy, on world peace. On graduation with the Associate of Arts Degree, I was awarded the Scholarship of the Kiwanis Foundation and I gained admission into California State College (now University) at Fullerton with offers of a track and a soccer scholarship, while I worked part-time (courtesy of the Shellers) from three weeks after my arrival in the United States, at Disneyland in Anaheim, California, to augment my resources. The advice to me by my senior brother, on my departure from Nigeria, not to abandon or trivialize my athletic and soccer abilities had become prophetic.

In the summer months of 1967, I initiated two important actions. First, I reviewed my life as I was wont to do on occasions, and felt that at twenty-four I should begin to think seriously of family life. My childhood sweetheart and neighbour with whom I had kept in touch since I departed Nigeria, readily came to mind. She was about completing her higher high school education at CHSA and would be seeking admission to college the following year. However, she had lost both of her parents -- the father in 1962 when she was fourteen (14) and her mother in 1966 when she was eighteen (18). Therefore, the decision-making process in this matter was not so simple or straightforward. I had known the family since 1953 and in fact the father was, believe it or not, my friend. In my young age I also ran several errands for the mother to whom my girlfriend was the only child. Our relationship was therefore well known to both of her parents but after their demise, a guardian whom I did not even remember ever meeting, was in control. My girlfriend who had seen me off at the Apapa Port when I departed Nigeria on January 14th, 1966, was agreeable to a university education in the U.S. but her guardian who was unsure of allowing an only child in his care indulge in such adventure, was very reluctant.

The guardian, a reputable lawyer of Sierra Leone extraction, rather than make enquiries with my family and/or College simply contended that the proceeds from her parents' properties could not support even the airfare.

My interest-free credit with the Sheller family and my own savings were readily available if only she would decide to take the risk of university education in the USA. We agreed that if she came, we would not rush into marriage but observe one another for about one year before deciding on marriage. The deal, guardian or no guardian, was sealed! Since she was to finish her high school education in December of 1967, she applied to the California State College at Fullerton for admission against the 1968/69 academic year.

The application and passport issuance processes were jinxed. I sent her the application form three different times. They kept getting lost in the mail. The duly filled application form suffered similar fate. Expectedly, the application for passport was not supported by the guardian therefore she had to be ingenious. Remembering that both her parents were originally from Sierra Leone, she approached the Sierra Leonean Embassy for a Sierra Leonean Passport, which she obtained with the help of her half-brother, Adewale Hamilton Rollings, who was resident in Freetown. We were now beginning to anticipate problem with the issuance of an American Visa. Therefore, as the passport drama played out, the Shellers sent an advance letter to the United States Embassy in Nigeria to facilitate the issuance of an American visa to Iyabo Gladys Knox-Rollings. The embassy immediately invited her to put in her visa application. Ironically, her passport was yet to be issued. She approached the embassy to explain the delay and was asked to submit her application anytime she was ready.

Another matter which agitated my mind in the summer of 1967 stemmed from the bad news from home that my mom and dad had finally separated. My senior brother, who was the first of seven children, conceived of a plan to salvage the educational prospects of the younger ones. He was to ensure they completed high school and I was to do whatever was possible to ensure they completed their university education in the United States. This plan was noble but my immediate junior sister married immediately after high school and her husband who became privy to this plan wrote to me of the need to exclude her from the plan as it would adversely affect his marriage. My senior brother and I considered it a reasonable request and therefore obliged. However, for reason of not causing disharmony in their family, we have not discussed this development till this day.

At a summer party of the Sheller and Gilbert families in the summer of 1967, I was approached by a College Professor at Bridgewater College, Virginia, with an offer of a full scholarship. I explained that I was already committed to California State College at Fullerton but we were nevertheless in correspondence for several months after. During this period, I mentioned my junior brother, Adewunmi, to him as a good substitute. He promptly agreed and requested his address which I very gladly provided. In a most stunning development, my girlfriend and my brother departed Lagos the same day and on the same flight through London for the United States. In London they parted ways, Adewunmi took a direct flight to the east coast and Iyabo, a polar flight to Los Angeles. They arrived in the United States in November 1968 by air, not by ship.

On my resumption at California State College at Fullerton, I moved from the Sheller home to a two-bedroom apartment which I shared with Duane Thomas and Dick Burner, who were members of the same athletics team with me. Iyabo, on her arrival, was gladly welcomed to my old room in the Sheller home. Soon after she arrived, she started addressing the Shellers as "mom" and "dad", an appellation which I had resisted on

27

the basis of colour because of the embarrassment it might cause in public. But here we were faced with the reality of life. After all that the Shellers had been to us, it was clear that our bond of relationship with them was colour neutral. Their grandson, Nathan (Hal's son), till this day calls me dad!

I obtained my B.A. Degree in Economics in the Spring Semester of 1969 and was granted admission by the Ivy League School, Claremont Graduate School in California, direct for a PhD degree in Economics beginning in the Fall Semester of the same year. On 17th March, 1969, Iyabo and I were engaged in a private ceremony at the West Whiting residence of the Shellers in Fullerton, California. The wedding was on 12th September of the same year.

Claremont was very, very, different in terms of quality standard required of the students and it was very expensive. I relied on my interest-free credit facility to meet my financial commitments in the first year and to purchase a replacement car when our first car became irreparable. In the second year, I was lucky to be among the recipients of the scholarship of the Lincoln School of Public Finance which more than covered all of my academic expenses. The savings were handy and used to help bring my junior sister, Omotunde, to start her university education in the United States. Now, there were only two more sisters to help! They were Olutowo and Olufunke.

Going through Claremont was rather difficult. I was stretched to the limit of my academic ability. The Comprehensive Examination was taken by thirteen (13) of us and only five of us were reported to have passed with two of the five having a re-sit. Mine was in Advanced Econometrics which I eventually passed with a B+ and successfully defended my thesis on 30th August, 1973. But there was a mild drama about this defence. My wife and I were scheduled for dinner at the Shellers' the same day and I did not want to be distracted by the concern of the family for the defence. I therefore ensured that none of them in the family was privy to it. At dinner I passed the letter inviting me for the defence to Mom Sheller and after reading through she exclaimed "It is today!" to which I answered in the affirmative while announcing my success. Claremont was now behind me and it was time to return home to Nigeria which event took place on the 19th of September, 1973 ---about seven and a half years from the date of my departure from Nigeria!!!

Higher Secondary School And University Education

At Comprehensive High School Aiyetoro

With Track Mates At Cal State Fullerton

Matriculation at University Of Ibadan

At A Track Meet With Musa Dogonyaro at Biola College California

CHAPTER 5

THE RETURN TO NIGERIA

In the winter of 1971/1972, I received a call from my Placement Centre, Claremont Graduate School, alerting me to an impending phone call from the Department of Economics, California State University, Northridge, for a possible teaching appointment. The call, which eventually came, was from the Head of Department, Professor James Esmay. He inquired about my interest in, and availability for, a teaching position on the faculty. An interview date and time were agreed upon. The interview turned out to be simply an interaction. I was merely introduced to other lecturers in the Department and was allocated classes -- first-year " Macroeconomics " and third-year "Money and Banking." We moved to Sepulveda in North Hollywood, and my wife was admitted for a post-graduate degree course in Hospital Administration, having obtained an undergraduate degree in Sociology at California State University, Fullerton.

In the academic year that I was at California State University, Northridge, my family became terribly home-sick and we started making plans to return home. I applied to the Universities of

Ibadan, Lagos and Ahmadu Bello. While the first two were still considering my application, Ahmadu Bello University (ABU) had offered me an appointment. I duly informed my Head of Department at Northridge, who was reluctant to see me leave and promised to reserve the position for me for one year just in case I did not like my position at home.

We wasted no time accepting the appointment at ABU and on 19th September, 1973, we arrived on a British Airways flight in Lagos to a warm and most surprising reception by a family delegation led by my father!!! This reception paved the way for reconciliation in the family. Mom and Dad were reconciled, and the family was back together again. All other women in my father's life were gone. Some of them were reported not to have said goodbye before leaving. Even my infamous uncle disappeared. We picked the pieces from there. We renovated the house and within a year we were all back in the family house.

ABU was intriguing in many ways. Quite a number of the lecturers such as Professor O' Connel and Professor Bambri who was Head of the Department of Economics had migrated from the University of Ibadan (UI). You will remember that Professor Bambri had been my tutorial lecturer at UI. At ABU, I taught second-year Macroeconomics, and Money and Banking. I was also a tutorial lecturer for first-year Macroeconomics which was taught by Professor Bambri. At ABU, a few incidents endeared me to the students. First, in my tutorial class, students inquired to know whether the "substitution effect" was positive or negative. They were confused by the fact that the various textbooks to which they had access were not unanimous on the subject. It was also reported that the recommended textbook, Economics by Robert G. Lipsey (simply referred to as Lipsey) which was an international authority on the subject had claimed that the "effect" was positive. It was one of those rare situations that students normally relish. But I was just coming from Graduate School and most of such details were on my fingertips. My reply that the substitution effect was always negative generated a prolonged debate which was not to be resolved until the next academic year when incidentally a new edition of "Lipsey" was published and it correctly reported the substitution effect as negative!

Second, in my Macroeconomics class, we examined quite a number of theories of consumption but the students were simply interested in which one was the acceptable theory -- that on which they were to concentrate on for the purpose of their examination. It was somewhat difficult to convince them that the consumption function for any country was usually unique. Since the Nigerian Government was at that time contemplating the payment of the Udoji Awards, which not only doubled salaries in the Public Service, but was to accommodate one year's salary arrears, the students were given a class assignment to predict what Nigerians were likely to do with the windfall they were to receive from the one-year Udoji Award using an appropriate consumption function. The result was discussed in class a few weeks before the award was paid. It predicted that Nigerians would spend virtually all of the arrears on consumption rather than save it. The class was pleasantly surprised when its prediction was correct as virtually all durable goods stores were emptied once the arrears were paid! It was incisive that even at their level, they could engage in meaningful policy analysis. I was deeply gratified.

A few months after we had settled in ABU, I received a letter (redirected to me from California, United States of America), signed by Dr. O. Teriba, requesting that I provide references in support of my application for employment with the Department of Economics, UI. My wife and I reviewed the situation against the background of the warm reception we had received in Zaria and decided not to oblige Ibadan. However, there were a few unsettling matters in ABU. The institution appeared to have difficulty fully internalizing/integrating Nigerians who were not of northern origin. For example, getting my most junior sister admitted into the School of Basic Studies or securing employment for my wife was like going through the eye of a needle. Even though my wife was eventually given an appointment in the Institute of Health as an Administrator, the appointment was on contract with far reaching implications for her career prospects. Additionally, our son whose health was somewhat fragile, had great difficulty adjusting to the harmattan dust. In the second academic session, we decided largely because of the last two reasons, to relocate to the southwest. In spite of these observations about ABU, however, when as we shall see later, my professional career experienced an existential threat, my northern professional colleagues/friends were more helpful, reliable, and faithful than most of the professional colleagues/ friends of my own ethnic group.

While at ABU, I developed an appetite for consultancy and the Nigerian Institute of Social and Economic Research (NISER) in Ibadan, was an attraction. The Institute advertised for positions in its consultancy outfit located in Lagos for which I applied and was shortlisted. The interview was the very first I was to attend in my professional career, so I really did not know what to expect. The interviewing panel was chaired by the Director of Research at the Central Bank of Nigeria, Dr. Adekunle, who was also a member of the NISER Governing Council. The panel included the Chairman of the Governing Council, and Professor H. M. A. Onitiri who was the Director (a position which is now designated as Director-General). A small drama played out when I disagreed with the Chairman of the interview on a major policy issue. The argument was so profound that I expressed the disappointment that there was no blackboard provided at the interview venue on which I could demonstratively prove the superiority of my argument. The Chairman was visibly uncomfortable, and it affected our relationship much later in life.

Instead of an appointment letter to the consultancy outfit I received two correspondences from NISER. The first was an invitation to an interview for the research outfit domiciled in Ibadan and for which I was informed that the Director General had expressed interest in having me associated with. The second was an invitation to a NISER conference in Ibadan, to present a paper on the very subject matter which was the contentious issue between me and the interview Chairman in Lagos. At the conference, I had the privilege of fully presenting my position before the highest caliber of professionals in the field and I was deeply gratified. It turned out that the interview Chairman had been newly recruited by the Central Bank of Nigeria from the International Monetary Fund (IMF) and that our disagreement stemmed largely from the traditional IMF view and that of mainstream economists. Nevertheless, one of my most nauseating professional weaknesses --snobbishness-- which I must have inculcated at Claremont, was beginning to clearly manifest.

I was emerging from the second NISER interview when the conference took place. The interview was chaired by someone else. It was smooth-sailing and I was offered an appointment which was one grade higher than what I had in ABU, Zaria. However, because both Professor H. M. A. Onitiri of NISER and Professor Bambri, my Head of Department in Zaria, had a long-standing relationship, it was agreed that I transit to NISER, Ibadan, at the end of the session rather than in the middle of it. The transition to Ibadan was, therefore, made at the end of 1974/1975 academic session. However, while I waited in Zaria,

35

it was agreed that I work on a number of NISER assignments, including representing the Director at international conferences and/or meetings.

Perhaps the most important event that brought me into the limelight took place at the Nigerian Economic Society Annual Conference held at the Bagawuda Lake Hotel in Kano in 1974.

My friend and colleague in ABU, Dr. (now Professor) J. S. Odama, requested that I substitute for him in discussing three papers that were scheduled for presentation at the afternoon session of the conference. He explained that his work as Assistant Secretary of the society did not allow him enough time to review the papers. I obliged and managed to go through the papers during lunch. The papers were by renowned members of the society-- Professor Ojetunji Aboyade, Department of Economics at the University of Ibadan, Professor Billy Joseph Stanley Dudley, Head of the Department of Political Science, University of Ibadan and Professor Bade Onimode also of the Department of Economics, University of Ibadan. The session was chaired by Mr. Gilbert Chikelu who was the Permanent Secretary of the Federal Ministry of Economic Planning. My review of the papers was very highly commended. Professor Aboyade exuberantly congratulated me and Professor Onitiri invited me to his Chalet for further discussion. Several other colleagues from all over the nation complimented me. It was most unusual that the compliment was going to the discussant and not the presenters!

It is very pertinent to mention here that Professor Aboyade and I crossed paths several times. The first time was in December, 1965 during the extra-moral athletics meeting at UI when I represented Tedder Hall in the high jump event. As the Chief Field Judge of the competition, he approached me with two bottles of Fanta while charging me to, at the next opportunity, ensure that I broke the existing university record of six feet six inches. My achievement at the athletics meeting was six feet three inches (though my personal best was six feet five inches) The British Empire and Commonwealth Games record at the time was six feet eleven inches and the Nigerian national record was six feet eight inches. The second encounter with Professor Ojetunji Aboyade was much later in life, in the early 1990's, when I led a group of industrialists in my capacity as head of a World Bank project, The Industrial Technical Assistance Project, to a meeting with the Presidential Advisory Committee at Dodan Barracks in Lagos. Professor Aboyade, who was Chairman of the Committee, immediately upon sighting me co-opted me into the Presidential Committee by disentangling me from the group which I had led to his Committee. Leadership of the group was then thrusted on Chief P.C. Asiodu who had famously been a Permanent Secretary and had recently joined the rank of indigenous captains of industry. Incidentally, the Secretary to the Government of the Federation, who was already quite familiar with my professional competence, made a scheduled appearance before the Committee on the same day. I am most certain that he went away wondering why and how someone who was not a statutory member of the Committee was fully participating in activities of the Committee!

CHAPTER 6

EXISTENTIAL THREATS

I assumed duty in NISER at the end of the 1974/1975 academic session but my stay there was anything but smooth. Most of my new colleagues were resentful of my appointment as Research Fellow I, as against Research Fellow II. The situation was aggravated by my appointment as head of a division in which capacity I was a member of the Management Committee, and by my close professional relationship with the Director who was deeply disparaged by the followership because he was thought by a powerful group of staff to have enjoyed an excessively long period of leadership at the Institute. I turned down an open invitation to conspiratorially disengage him, and the animosity against me boiled over when in the year following my assumption of duty, I was recommended for accelerated promotion to the position of Senior Research Fellow. Five members of staff were reported to have been so aggrieved that they relied on the U.I regulation which provided for staff to put themselves up for promotion, to do so. On the very day of the meeting of the NISER Appointments and Promotions Committee, the Director consulted with me and thereafter withdrew his recommendation. This was a master stroke as the petitions of the five adversaries no longer had any basis in fact.

Soon after the conclusion of the promotion exercise, the

Institute advertised for various positions including the one to which I would have been promoted. I applied and was successful, but the interview result had to be approved by the University of Ibadan Appointments and Promotions (A&P) Committee and there were veiled threats it would never happen. However, before the scheduled meeting of the University A&P, the 1977 Decree of NISER was promulgated. It established NISER as an autonomous entity. Thus, empowering the Institute to be its own final arbiter in the promotion of its staff. The Institute then turned down the invitation of the University A&P which had been fortuitously scheduled to take place only a few days after the decree was promulgated. My appointment as Senior Research Fellow was approved by the NISER Governing Council at its next meeting!

NISER offered me a unique opportunity to develop my potentials to the fullest. It gave me both national and international exposure as I represented Professor Onitiri and the Institute at various meetings/conferences in and out of the country. This helped me to distinguish myself as authority in a number of special areas which included Inflation, The Economic Community of West African States (ECOWAS), and model building.

However, throughout my career I had to contend, at every turn, with adversaries who were unrelenting. On occasions, I reflected on how I had come to earn so much respect from colleagues but very little affection. My analysis, which is based on comments from both objective and not so objective sources, is intriguing. Some considered me to be conceited, citing my arrogance at the respective interviews for the NISER Consultancy in Lagos and at the Research outfit of the Institute in Ibadan. In one particular instance, a reviewer of my papers for professorship confided in a colleague that his assessment of my papers would be negative because I was too pompous. He complained that I did not regularly visit the Social Science Faculty of the University of Ibadan coffee-room to have tea with professional colleagues. I did not heed the advice of the colleague, who was privy to this accusation, to initiate a rapprochement with the reviewer. Needless to say, the assessor carried out his threat.

Given the benefit of hindsight, the accusation of conceitedness and snobbishness are not totally unfounded. I think I had cultivated them at Claremont Graduate School especially. After obtaining my PhD, I confided in my wife that there was no way I was going to be able to apply in life, ten percent of what I had learnt at Claremont. Additionally, I had started very early in life (secondary school) to read books of biographies and philosophies, and I had always tried to be all-knowing. However, even after this realization, I did not let this perception of me distract me except that it instilled in me the attitude of being somewhat introverted.

There is also my principled stand on "deals" beginning with the open refusal to be involved in the conspiratorial disengagement of Professor H. M. A. Onitiri and the refusal of a *quid pro quo* arrangement on the publication of a book. There was also the refusal to step down my comments on an article published in a professional journal even after the author had passionately pleaded with me to do so. More damning was the decision to co-ordinate the elaboration of a macro-econometric model for the Nigerian economy under the auspices of the Federal Ministry of Economic Planning. I was unaware that there had been several failed attempts at executing this project because of inability to reach acceptable agreements with those at the University of Ibadan and University of Ife (now Obafemi Awolowo University). Unknown to me, the Ministry had a preference for me largely because of the erudition I had recently demonstrated and, more importantly, because I was in the employment of its most reputable parastatal. I was supported by the Permanent

41

Secretary with every conceivable facility and resource to complete the assignment. When it was completed, the Ministry sought the assistance of the United Nations Development Programme (UNDP) to assess the output alongside several other models including the World Bank Model, which had earlier been built for the Ministry. The assessor was also to recommend which model was to be used for both short-term and long-term planning in Nigeria. The verdict of the assessor, Professor O.G Wadstead, published in "A Framework for Prospective Plan on Nigeria and its attendant Planning Systems (1987)" concluded on pages 92 and 93 and I quote: "I find that the NISER Model is much better adapted than the RMSM Model (of the World Bank) to guide policy in Nigeria at present. The objections I have to the RMSM Model do not apply to the NISER Model." "Even as it stands, I consider it a useful tool for short-term planning, given its aspects of production, consumption, and institutional policies which comprises the economy".

The Ministry was so delighted in this outcome that it sent several of its officers to NISER for training on how to operationalise the model. This monumental achievement inadvertently expanded the scope of my adversaries/detractors. Therefore, as soon as my detractors gained support in the Ministry, they jettisoned the pursuit of operationalising the model and initiated action to building of a new and comparable model which effort has failed to come to fruition even now, some thirty-three years after.

Another reason advanced by some of my adversaries was the coincidence of thought which often played out at the NISER management meetings between Professor Onitiri and I. Since I was the most junior in rank of the members of the Management Committee, I was invariably the last to be called upon to express opinion on critical issues of policy. Thereafter, the Director would review the contributions and pronounce on the management's decision. It turned out that the pronouncements very often echoed my contributions. This tended to give the impression that I was either a tool of the Executive or that the Director and I had constituted ourselves into an inner caucus. I was so concerned about this development that I made a special trip to Lagos to consult with my mother. She listened to me attentively and explained to me that there was nothing I could do about it because the views of those who are endowed with knowledge and understanding are generally identical if not the same. Her explanation was very reassuring.

My adversaries mapped out two strategies to deal with me. The first, was to ensure that I did not earn the title of Professor, and the second was to ensure that I was not given exposure. Information filtered to me through reliable sources, on both. On the latter, a director in the Ministry of National Planning, Mr. Akin Adegbayo, openly chided the Director-General of the National Centre for Economic Management and Administration (NCEMA), now defunct, for giving me a prominent role at a national conference on Inflation. Mr. Adegbayo's concern was correct because on the following day, the editorial of The Champion Newspaper, beginning on its front page, drew the attention of the government to my paper. The undiscerning would think that this heinous animosity was pointless. Nevertheless, it was real and very formidable.

I was tremendously blessed with a number of safety valves in my arduous professional career. As the drama of promotion/appointment to the position of Senior Research Fellow played out, NISER conceived of a programme to assist each of the various states of the federation with a study of the resources available to them for development and to advise on how to exploit these resources. I was assigned Lagos State. The survey which commenced in 1978 was concluded in 1979. This was just in time for the change-over from the military to the civilian administration. I received tremendous support for my survey of Lagos State from the Head of Service, Dr. Olufemi Lewis and from Mr. Babatunde Fanimokun, a longtime friend and classmate at the Comprehensive High School Aiyetoro.

When the survey report was ready, I made silent copies available to both Dr. Lewis and Mr. Fanimokun. Unknown to me, the newly elected Executive Governor, Alhaji Lateef Jakande, of the state had access to the 196-page report and perused it following which he invited me for a discussion. The Commissioner for Economic Planning and Land Matters, Honourable Hundeyin of Badagry and the Permanent Secretary, Mr. Oguntimehin from Epe, were present and Mr. Odunsi, an administrative officer in the Ministry, covered the meeting. The Governor opened the discussion by disclosing that he knew I was a Lagosian and would wish I assisted his government. I requested to know what precisely he wanted me to attend to. He did not immediately reply but talked about the ministry in which I would be domiciled and what facilities would be at my disposal. Pressed again for what exactly I was to assist with, he replied: "If you could do for Lagos State something comparable to the book you wrote about the State, that will be sufficient." I was deeply gratified that he had read my book and had found it to be profoundly relevant for policy. This was just the type of contribution I had hoped, soon after I obtained my PhD in Economics, that I would make to the development of my country. The Governor formalized his request for my release for one year in the first instance, to NISER. Professor Onitiri was now on a United Nations Assignment on Zimbabwe, and Mr. Basil Igwe was holding fort. Management under his leadership resisted the idea. However, when pressure from the Lagos State Government became difficult to ignore, I was released for one year in the first instance on condition that my salary would be remitted in advance to NISER and that my period of absence would not count towards my years of service in NISER. This was in spite of the fact that NISER was set up to serve both the State and Federal Governments.

I assumed duty in Lagos State in January of 1980 and was designated Secretary for Planning and Executive Secretary of the Economic Planning Board. I was to reorganize the Economics Wing of the Ministry of Economic Planning and Land Matters from one department to four, collate and consolidate all policy papers of the Unity Party of Nigeria into the 1981-1985 Economic Development Plan of Lagos State, monitor and produce quarterly reports on all projects in the Development Plan, and to co-ordinate under the leadership of a Chairman of the Economic Planning Board, Dr. Abisogun Leigh, the development plans of the Local Government which plans respectively derived from the State Plan. The Development Plan was launched on schedule and I was allocated ten newly bought vehicles to ensure effective monitoring of plan implementation. The quarterly reporting of the monitoring was so effective that the Governor prevailed on me to present monthly reports as well. My explanation to him that implementors needed some time to improve on the implementation of their projects fell on deaf ears. I obliged him and he confided in one of my bosses that "no one could lie to him any more" on the stage(s) of implementation of projects. In December, 1981 when I informed the Governor of my intention to return to NISER he was very reluctant to let me go. After he was persuaded that a prolonged stay could jeopardize my professional career, he requested that I recommend to him someone else in NISER to succeed me.

Before my exit in February 1982, I, at the instance of Professor Onitiri, secured an allocation of land in Victoria Island for a regional office for NISER. The regional office was never built. Indeed, my investigation indicates that the allocation has been disposed of and that the proceeds from the disposal has been a subject of speculation in NISER for over decades. I returned to my regular work in NISER but was due for sabbatical in 1983. There was therefore the need to plan for where I was going to spend my sabbatical and what to do during the period. I decided on the Department of Economics, University of Ibadan and was given appointment in October, 1983 as Associate Professor which title was in later years changed to Reader.

However, it appeared that my rendezvous with destiny did not include direct affinity with UI as I received a few days later, a telex message from the United Nations Institute for Development and Economic Planning (IDEP) in Dakar, Senegal, offering me a teaching appointment. This latter offer was certainly preferable. So, I approached the then Head of Department at U. I. and intimated to him of my dilemma. We both agreed that the United Nations offer was preferable.

On 31st October, 1983, I arrived in Dakar and assumed duty on November 2, since November 1st was a public holiday there. My three-year stay in Dakar was particularly rewarding. My Daily Subsistence Allowance (DSA) which for some unexplained reason was paid to me for nine months instead of one, was enough not only to settle me down but was for one month sufficient to buy a brand-new car (Toyota crown) because United Nations Employees do not pay tax on purchases of durable goods such as cars. The salary which I received along with the DSA, while it lasted, was even more handsome. I did not buy a car. Instead, I used the opportunity to save for my children to attend summer school abroad in each of the years that I was in that employment, and for their eventual education abroad. I filled all of my financial potholes and more. My father passed on in November of 1983 and the burial and funeral ceremonies were financially most convenient. The land which I had bought from my father and which was under construction but was abandoned since I returned to NISER, Ibadan, received attention and construction did not stop until completion. When after I became King, and there was need to build another palace, the savings was more than sufficient to put it in place.

On the completion of my assignment in Dakar, I bought household equipment such as a gas cooker, state of the art electronic equipment, and a refrigerator. I transported them home by air. I also bought a set of furniture which I transported home by sea. It was absolutely, unbelievably rewarding.

While in Dakar, the molestation by my professional colleagues continued unabated. The NISER regulation required that I should return to NISER immediately after the one year of my sabbatical. However, there was already a precedent of one Dr. Sylvanus Okpala who had been similarly engaged by a United Nations Agency in Ethiopia. No pressure was put on him to return to NISER. Even after I had bargained with the Acting Director-General (Dr. Akin Adubifa) that I was not going to compete with him for the Director-General's position which was then vacant, there was no reprieve. The Acting Director-General was in Dakar on a consultancy assignment and had stayed with me in my four bed-room villa, complete with a garage and boys' quarters. A few days after his departure from Dakar, I received a telex message from NISER giving me an ultimatum to return to my duty post in NISER or my appointment would be terminated. It turned out that Professor 'Poju Onibokun (now of blessed memory), who was acting for the Acting Director-General had summoned a management meeting in his absence, to issue the ultimatum. I appreciated the explanation but decided that push had come to shove. I made a trip home, consulted with my wife and personally submitted my resignation letter. I concluded that, after all, the one-year salary that might be demanded of me was easily affordable. The Acting Director-General accepted my resignation but had to inform both the Honourable Minister and the Permanent Secretary. Both overruled his acceptance of my resignation and charged the successor Director-General who eventually was Professor Dotun Phillips, to ensure my reabsorption into NISER. In November, 1986, Professor Phillips invited me for negotiation. I was very reluctant to enter into any discussion about returning to NISER largely because I already had an assurance of a respectable job in Geneva, Switzerland, courtesy of Professor H. M. A. Onitiri. In this difficult time, my bosom friend, who had followed the NISER debacle with keen interest and was my confidant, Mr. Oyeniyi Akande, advised that we discuss the matter with Professor Onitiri who was undoubtedly my mentor. Professor Onitiri advised that in view of the intervention of both the Minister and Permanent Secretary, I should return to NISER.

In February, 1987, I resumed in NISER with all conciliatory measures made by NISER. During my December 19, 1986 interaction with the new Director-General, Professor Dotun Phillips, he intimated to me that the Federal Ministry of Industries had successfully negotiated a technical assistance programme with the World Bank and had requested NISER to recommend a Director/Head. The project, Industrial Technical Assistance Project (ITAP), was to be domiciled in NISER, Ibadan, as the Policy Analysis Department (PAD). He offered this Directorship to me. However, the NISER Consultancy Unit in Lagos was actually interested in housing the project since it was already serving the same Federal Ministry of Industries. If this expectation was realized, the Ministry would now have two departments domiciled in NISER. But I was unaware that the Ministry had served notice that it was no longer interested in the NISER Consultancy Unit. Therefore, on my assumption of duty as Director, PAD, in February, 1987, I had to contend with a disintegrating Consultancy Unit whose staff looked up to me for empathy and when I could not provide any succour,

I was deemed a destroyer. The ITAP was to recruit its own staff, professional and nonprofessional, including its own administrative staff. Its funding was separate from NISER's.

Additionally, the project was to be supported by a firm of foreign consultants who were to be shortlisted by the World Bank and interviewed by the Director and some senior officials of the Ministry. Virtually all aspects of the project's establishment and function were a potential source of conflict with NISER. In order to allow for smoothness of operation, we put in place a procedure which required our accountant, and internal auditor to process all purchases/transactions through the NISER structure. I reserved the authority to approve purchases/transactions while payment was effected by NISER. The World Bank, however, would recognize only the approval of the Director for all foreign exchange transactions and for the payment of the six foreign consultants who each earned $15,000.00 monthly. The replenishment of funds by the World Bank was, however, predicated on the Bank's approval of the external auditor's report.

The Policy Analysis Department (PAD), as the project was known in NISER, was required to prepare for Nigeria a new tariff book which was to be launched in the budget speech of Mr. President in January 1989. The assignment also included the elaboration of a number of macroeconomic models namely, Computable General Equilibrium Model, Input Output Table and a System Dynamics Model. Under a separate assistance provided by the United Nations Industrial Development Organisation (UNIDO), PAD was to prepare an Industrial Master Plan otherwise referred to as "Strategic Management of Industrial Development" similar to the one adopted by the Asian Tigers. There was also the technical training in these special fields, which was supported by the United Nations Development Programme (UNDP) and the European Union

(EU). Funding was not a problem but the procedure for release was stringent requiring very strict conditions all of which bothered on transparency. This assignment required that we assemble the most capable professionals mindful of Federal Character. Through the effort of the Honourable Minister, we secured the release of Dr. (now Professor) Ode Ojowu from the Centre for Development Studies, University of Jos, to oversee the preparation of the Industrial Master Plan; Dr. (now Professor) Mike Kwanashie of ABU. to oversee the training Programme of the UNDP; Professor Femi Kayode of the Department of Economics, University of Ibadan to take charge of the training programme of the European Union, and Mr. Lawrence L. Arinola to supervise data collection and analysis. We also set up a small intelligence network to monitor the foreign consultants whose submissions to me needed to be cross checked because of the security implications for the economy of setting very low tariffs and creating a floodgate for importation which would negatively affect domestic production of goods in which we had comparative advantage.

We collected detailed information from the Federal Office of Statistics (now the National Bureau of Statistics). Indeed, the most recent questionnaires retrieved from the National Industrial Survey were photocopied in their entirety ready for collation and processing. The intended activities for the PAD were monstrous. The facilities at NISER were grossly inadequate such that an elaborate plan for rented office and residential accommodation became imperative. All of the activities were to commence simultaneously because no donor agency, except the EU, was willing to delay implementation. However, because of the January deadline for the new tariff book, this assignment was given topmost priority.

It took a while to conclude arrangements for the foreign consultants to be in place, especially, for their residential accommodation. Once these matters were resolved and they assumed duty, the consultants confided in me that the January deadline for the launching of the new tariff book was not feasible. There were no computers to work with and the World Bank procurement process would take a little over a month. Additionally, the thousands of questionnaires which we had photocopied had not been coded, compiled or processed in any way. Even the compilation would require that a programme be written and tested. In the midst of this dismal picture, I contacted one of my students at Ahmadu Bello University who was now teaching at the Faculty of Social Sciences, UI, and he recommended to me Mr. Layi L. Arinola, a computer guru, who he assured me was up to the task of ensuring we met the deadline. I invited Mr. Arinola to the PAD and briefed him thoroughly on our predicament. The leader of the foreign consultants, Mr. Robinson, who was in attendance was not persuaded that the data processing work could be quickly concluded. He appeared to be mindful of the reputation of his firm, and insisted on meeting the Honourable Minister, Lt General Alani Akinrinade.

At the meeting with the Minister, the consultants, referencing the Word Bank, reiterated their position that all matters relating to data availability could not be resolved in less than six months. Expectedly the Honourable Minister expressed regret but sought my opinion on what could be done. I assured the Honourable Minister that we could resolve all issues relating to the data in less than three months. I did not think anybody believed me but the Minister encouraged us to make the effort. On the advice of Mr. Arinola, since I had relative control over the counterpart funding provided by the Ministry but domiciled with NISER, we rented nine computers from a firm in Lagos, engaged and trained eighteen students of the University of Ibadan who coincidentally were on holidays, to work three shifts a day on the data entry and compilation. Mr. Arinola wrote the software required and in three weeks, to everyone's amazement, all of

51

the data issues had been resolved. In the time that was left before the January, 1989 deadline, the Effective Protection Rate for each of the commodities imported into Nigeria, the Computable General Equilibrium model and the input-output models which were required for policy simulation were all ready and available. The NISER macro-econometric model was also available for short-term forecasting and analysis. In the months ahead, I proudly drafted a speech for a public address by the Vice President, Rear Admiral Augustus Aikhomu, heralding to manufacturers and the country at large, the introduction of a new tariff book in the 1989 budget speech. I subsequently drafted the relevant input for the budget speech itself.

The elaboration of an Industrial Master Plan was also a Herculean task. Government had to set up a private sector committee to liaise between PAD and the industrial sector because the industrial sector had to be carried along every step of the way. Mr. Rasheed Gbadamosi, who was at the time the Chairman of the Board of the Nigerian Industrial Development Bank (NIDB), was its chairman.

There was the necessity not only to sensitize those in the private sector but also those in the public sector on the need for such a plan and on the respective roles that were to be played by each of them in the elaboration of the Plan. Dr. (Now Professor) Ode Ojowu who had graduated with a first-class degree in Economics in ABU, Zaria did a marvelous job conceptualising the plan. His use of the input-output table to determine the bottlenecks in the Nigerian Economy was most revealing. The bottlenecks, in descending order, included Engineering, Petrochemicals, and Agro-Allied industries. His findings which were made late into the night (at about 10 p.m.) generated as much interest as controversy.

Over the next few days, the calculations were repeated over and over again. When consensus was finally reached, and the results were eventually made public at an elaborate stakeholders meeting, the conceptualization was so well received that it generated the agitation for the setting up, in the Ministry of Science and Technology, the National Agency for Science and Engineering Infrastructure (NASENI) which would be the first step to alleviating the engineering constraint in the Nigerian economy. This cause was championed by Dr. Timothy I. Obiagba who was the Director (Engineering) in the Federal Ministry of Science and Technology at the time and who was in attendance at the stakeholders meeting.

The next most important recommendation from this report was the determination of the sequence in which industrial development should take place and the classification of these industries into clusters (or sub-systems). All industries in Nigeria were therefore classified and constituted into sub-systems on which there were representatives of the relevant ministries. The strategy for development of each sub-system and the support required from government were clearly articulated in the report prepared for each sub-system. There were twelve such reports. On August 4, 1989, the final report of the Industrial Master Plan otherwise known as "Strategic Management of Industrial Development" was submitted to Mr. President, General Ibrahim Gbadamosi Babangida, in his Abuja office.

The training programmes of the PAD commenced as soon as money was released for them. They were intended to be in-house and hands-on and were for nominees from both the public and private sectors. There were also foreign components of the training even though they were short-term in nature -- some three to six months.

In all of our assignments, there were quite a number of challenges. There were essentially four problems associated with our foreign consultants. First, based on intelligence report, the *curriculum vitae* of each of the consultants had been doctored to meet our requirements, the team leader, Mr. Robinson, was actually not an employee of the firm of Maxwell Stamps Associates which was awarded the contract. Unknown to us, the consulting firm was working under instructions to ensure that the tariff determination favoured the importation of goods, not domestic production. This required the statistical manipulation of the estimated tariffs. Second, because of foreign exchange variations, payment in foreign currency became murky.

The foreign consulting firm and the desk officers at the World Bank were pressurizing the Director of PAD to approve more monthly payments than was thought by the Director to be justified. Until I had this experience, I had always believed that the World Bank was impeccable. Well, I was grossly in error. I requested intelligence report on the foreign consulting firm and, to my surprise, even though the firm had been shortlisted, recommended and approved by the World Bank for the project, evidence provided by the Registrar of Companies in Britain showed that the consulting firm was not even in existence at the time that it was awarded the contract by the World Bank. In view of the persistence for more pay and the danger which my non-compliance posed to my reputation, I briefed the Honourable Minister who then took the matter up with the President of the World Bank. The contract was in consequence terminated and the desk officers at the World Bank disciplined and redeployed away from the project. We continued work on the project with one foreign consultant who was willing to remain on our own terms, and with Nigerian substitutes.

There were two other dimensions to the challenges. They relate to NISER and the Federal Ministry of Industries. All contracts and transactions that were awarded using funds provided as counterpart funding were initiated and approved by me, for payment through NISER. I had no authority on how and when payments were made and all vendors were alerted to this reality and appeared comfortable with it. However, it was the period of the Structural Adjustment Programme (SAP) and there was suddenly a seeming interest in NISER, in the foreign exchange component to which the "Deputy" Permanent Secretary and I were signatories. Interest developed in several other quarters in this pie. Additionally, the PAD was becoming so impactful that its reports were being cited by the World Bank. I was summoned to NISER and two directives were issued. The more troubling was that I should prepare grounds for the appropriation of the PAD by NISER. I was informed that the Honourable Minister would cooperate. The second directive related to the desire for foreign exchange. However, the Director-General was appreciative of the difficulty of dipping hands into the till therefore, he preferred that I put into effect a creaming arrangement with the consultants.

I knew that both directives would not fly either with the World Bank, whose relationship with NISER had been historically tenuous, and the Ministry which was beginning to showcase its own achievements. I contacted the Honourable Minister only on the issue of appropriation and he admonished me to ignore it. He remarked that the Director-General of NISER was already growing some "maggots" in his head. I also ignored the directive on creaming. When it became manifestly clear that I was not going to oblige NISER, the Director-General contacted the Ministry of his intention to change the Director of PAD in the tradition in which headship in the Institution was rotated. He identified as my replacement, an ebullient junior colleague.

There had now been a cabinet reshuffle and the new minister (Air Vice Mashal Mohammed Yahaya) was duly briefed by his predecessor even about the intended appropriation by NISER. The new Minister summoned me to his Lagos office for a meeting. In a very unusual manner, our meeting was very brief. He directed that I should stop sending advance copies of PAD's reports to the Director-General of NISER who he claimed, had been using them for policy advise to the Secretary to the Government of the Federation (SGF) and Mr. President. Secondly, he intimated to me his intention to move the PAD to Abuja. I thanked him for our good relationship and the confidence which he reposed in me but I explained that the movement to Abuja would mean an end to my involvement in the PAD since I was a *bona fide* staff of NISER. However, he had it all figured out. He was going to request for my secondment to the Ministry for two years in the first instance. So it was that PAD relocated to Abuja.

The Industrial Master Plan posed a different problem. As soon as the UNIDO funding was available, I nominated Professor Ode Ojowu to be the UNIDO consultant. Unknown to me, the Chairman of the Industrial Master Plan Committee (Alhaji Rashid Gbadamosi), which Committee was set up by the Ministry to facilitate contact with the private sector, had his own preferred candidate, Dr. Uma Eleazu, for the position. The Honourable Minister, who was not properly briefed on the matter, had been persuaded to accept the latter's nominee. The Honourable Minister summoned me to Abuja and requested that I bring along Professor Ojowu. On our arrival at the meeting, we were surprised to find the following were already seated for the meeting: the UNIDO representative in Nigeria, two UNIDO desk officers from Vienna, Austria, Mr. Rashid Gbadamosi, Chairman of the Industrial Master Plan Committee set up by the government, and Dr. Uma Eleazu. Please note that we had not been briefed as to the purpose of the meeting.

The Honourable Minister literally charged into the meeting venue. He explained that he was duly informed that I was seeking to replace Dr. Uma Eleazu whom he had approved for the consultancy position in UNIDO with someone else. I explained that in terms of qualification, Professor Ojowu was far superior, being a reputable economist whose release from the University of Jos the Minister had obtained from the University's Vice Chancellor for exactly the position in dispute. I also argued that Professor Ojowu had graduated with a first-class degree in Economics from Ahmadu Bello University and was my student. As for Dr. Uma Eleazu, I informed the Minister that he was a Political Scientist who had been teaching in the Black Studies Programme at the University of California in the US since his graduation. I concluded by saying my interest in Professor Ojowu was largely because the Minister had impressed to me that he wanted good quality job. A minor drama then played out. The Minister had been persuaded that I was showing preference for Professor Ojowu (whom the Minister had never met) because he was my clan's man. Notice that his name sounds Yoruba. Realizing that Professor Ojowu was his own clan's man rather than mine, the Minister posed the following question to Professor Ojowu who was sitting directly opposite him at the conference table: "Ode, are we not from the same tribe"? Ode did not answer until the question had been posed a third time. His reply was " I am not here on the basis of tribe!" I thought all hell was going to break loose, but it did not. The Honourable Minister thanked me for teaching their son to be a good economist but maintained his position on Dr. Uma Eleazu while nevertheless pleading with all of us to do a good quality job.

A strategy meeting was held by all of those who were at the meeting with the Honourable Minister soon after. A number of conceptual issues needed to be explained/clarified at the meeting and Professor Ojowu rightly deferred to Dr. Eleazu who expectedly had no clue. The UNIDO team had dinner with the Honourable Minister that evening. The following morning, I was invited for an early morning meeting with the Honourable

Minister. He confided in me that at the instance of the UNIDO desk officers in Vienna, he was reversing himself and Professor Ojowu should be the one in charge of the Industrial Master Plan. UNIDO was to find some other accommodation for Dr. Eleazu. I expressed apprehension in convincing Ode and he retorted: " But he was your student." Professor Ojowu was very quiet after I told him the outcome of my surprise meeting with the Honourable Minister. After a long silence we both assessed the situation to be a monumental victory for us.

The PAD moved to Abuja in 1991. Office accommodation was good but residential accommodation, though newly completed, was deplorable and inadequate. The plumbing work was simply atrocious. Two major events adversely affected our movement. First, the Permanent Secretary of the Ministry, Malam. A.S. Mohammed, died in an auto accident a few months before the movement, and second, there was a cabinet reshuffle and therefore a new Minister -- General Bagudu Mamman. Also worthy of note was the fact that the Director-General of NISER, whom we now were contending with, had established very strong connection in government, having prepared the much talked about Civil Service Reform. Combined with this development was the hostile environment in the Ministry where there were demands from various quarters to benefit from the foreign account of PAD. I offered to support overseas training of several months to those concerned and I made available a brand-new Peugeot 504 to the desk officer, but the preference by all, except one, was for me to dip hands into the till. In the final analysis, the feeling of frustration on their part led to a decision to kill the project. While this decision was most undesirable from the point of view of the national interest and the efforts which had gone into establishing the outfit, a decision such as this coming from the Directors, the Permanent Secretary and the then Honourable Minister had no chance of reversal. Even the expressed willingness of the World Bank to continue with the project fell on deaf ears. I set in motion the machinery for my staff to be absorbed into the mainstream of the Ministry and in the space of three months, I handed over the defunct project to the Ministry's Dr. Jemita who was head of the committee charged with the responsibility to supervise its demise. Good riddance!!!

CHAPTER 7

THE PROVERBIAL NINE LIVES

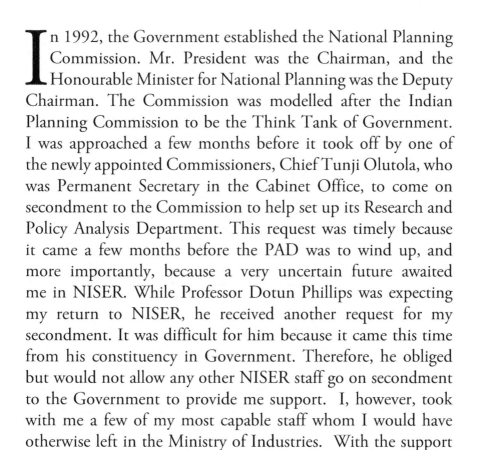

In 1992, the Government established the National Planning Commission. Mr. President was the Chairman, and the Honourable Minister for National Planning was the Deputy Chairman. The Commission was modelled after the Indian Planning Commission to be the Think Tank of Government. I was approached a few months before it took off by one of the newly appointed Commissioners, Chief Tunji Olutola, who was Permanent Secretary in the Cabinet Office, to come on secondment to the Commission to help set up its Research and Policy Analysis Department. This request was timely because it came a few months before the PAD was to wind up, and more importantly, because a very uncertain future awaited me in NISER. While Professor Dotun Phillips was expecting my return to NISER, he received another request for my secondment. It was difficult for him because it came this time from his constituency in Government. Therefore, he obliged but would not allow any other NISER staff go on secondment to the Government to provide me support. I, however, took with me a few of my most capable staff whom I would have otherwise left in the Ministry of Industries. With the support of these staff, I was able to complete one or two assignments, especially the 57x57 input-output table which, as far has was known then, was the largest from primary data.

Things were murky in the Commission. The other directors, nine of them, were uncertain of their positions because their profiles did not fit the positions they were occupying. The positions were rather designed for academics who were to be attracted from the University with a salary structure which allowed for twenty-five percent over and above the University scale. I appeared to them as the forerunner of this crop of professionals while they were destined to return to the mainstream Civil Service. Their efforts were therefore directed at returning the Commission to the mainstream Civil Service but to nevertheless earn the much higher salary. The Commission was therefore not an environment in which I enjoyed the camaraderie of the directors. Two of them, Mr. Akin Adegbayo and Mr. Christopher C. Chukwurah, were particularly hostile. I have already mentioned that the former was heard openly taking issues with the organizer of a conference for giving me exposure by inviting me to present a paper at a national conference. The latter was author of a document recommending, without any basis in fact, that the Department which I was invited to set up be scrapped. I was flabbergasted. Ironically at the end of my secondment to the Commission, this Director who wanted it scrapped was redeployed to head the same Department he had wanted scrapped. However, since NISER was a parastatal under the Commission, he was much later to be a member of the NISER Governing Council where he was better situated to deal a mortal blow not just to the Department I had set up but also to my career. But man proposes and God disposes.

The situation in the commission got a lot murkier because, in my position at the Commission, I was Chairman of the body before whom NISER and other parastatals were to defend their capital budgets. Naturally, NISER was concerned that I might not be fair dealing with their requests and sought the intervention of the Commissioner whom they had obliged in agreeing to my secondment. An epic battle that would last from 1995 to 2004 was beginning to unravel. My two-year secondment to the Commission was about to come to an end and there was a request to NISER for renewal. NISER was unsure how to respond largely because the Head of the Commission was also in the Director-General's constituency.

The situation was in this state of flux when I received a phone call from Dr. (now Professor) Ojowu sternly warning against my immediate return to NISER. He warned of an existential threat. He also intimated to me that a vacancy existed in the Presidency for someone with my profile. This was the National Economic Intelligence Committee (NEIC) headed by Professor Sam Adepoju Aluko. The Secretary and the eyes and ears of the Head of State and Commander-in-Chief (C-in-C) was Major General Garba Mohammed who, until this posting, was the Governor of Niger State. The Committee's membership was based on zonal representation and it reported directly to the C-in-C. Professor Ojowu argued that this would be a safe haven (my Egypt) until the ill will in NISER subsided. He added, however, that he was a member of the Committee and that I would be in the secretariat which would tantamount to a reversal of roles as we had known it in PAD. Sure, I needed Egypt!!! Professor Dotun Phillips was closing in and was unrelenting in doing so. I accepted this offer of assistance, and the following day, I received a directive from the Secretary to the Government of the Federation (SGF.), Under Flying Seal (UFS), to report in the Presidency "with immediate effect " to help set up the Research Department of NEIC

Professor Phillips was unavailable in NISER, Ibadan, and was to be away for a few days when the letter was delivered. Not minding that he already had the original which, by regulation, he was to hand over to me without hinderance, I left him a note and departed for Abuja where I concluded all formalities, including being placed on the payroll. My secondment had been financially rewarding largely because I carried with me everywhere I went, the University Scale. But at NEIC, it was even better as I was also entitled to a non-taxable allowance that was equivalent to my gross salary. A few days after I had concluded these formalities, I returned to NISER to personally see Professor Phillips and to review the new development with him. However, before my arrival in Ibadan I had rejuvenated my intelligence network at NISER and the first intelligence report was that documents had been prepared for the termination of my appointment and that instructions had been given to the Accounts Unit to prepare my gratuity and three months' salary in lieu of notice. Payment was to be made into my salary account in Ibadan. The war which had been simmering for years has now been finally declared. Professor Dotun Phillips was not one to be taken lightly for reason which had been stated earlier. He had declared a war which I could only fight if I shrewdly mobilized forces in Abuja. But first and foremost, I would have to clearly demonstrate to the forces in Abuja that I was not fighting the establishment. The epic war had started and I made my second move while at Ibadan by closing my salary account as Professor Dotun Phillips was still waiting to schedule a meeting of management to rubber stamp his recommendation. I returned to Abuja to prepare for a war that would be fought ONLY by defending oneself. No offense!!!

Some weeks later, having failed to make payment into my salary account, I received in the mail a letter terminating my appointment and forwarding two cheques, one for my gratuity and the other for three months' salary in lieu of notice. After due consultations in NEIC and the Office of the SGF, I returned the cheques to NISER drawing attention to the fact that I was still in service and drawing my regular salary from the Presidency and that the payment of gratuity and three months' salary in lieu of notice was premature and against extant Public Service Regulations. The Secretary to the Government of the Federation (SGF) fumed at this development and citing this as a second act of insubordination by the Director-General of NISER, he intimated to the Head of NEIC his intention to fire the Director -General of NISER. However, on the intervention of the Head of NEIC who did so without eliciting any concession from the NISER Director-General, the SGF's action was suspended. This had far reaching implications for my struggle. My support from the core North suddenly waned as this was considered a Yoruba internecine war. Unfortunately, the SGF, Alhaji Aminu Saleh was soon replaced by Alhaji Gidado Idris.

At some point in the struggle, the Head of NEIC confided in the Secretary of the Committee that I be returned to NISER to face the music. The Secretary called me in, intimated this privileged conversation to me and assured me it would never happen because he was convinced of my innocence and forthrightness. The irony of the position of a man from the core North and the one from my own ethnic group.

It never rains but pours! Soon after this effort by the Head of NEIC, Professor Samuel Aluko, I received a phone call from a longtime friend, Mr. Fatoki of the National Planning Commission. He was inquiring to know if I was aware that my confidential reports at the NEIC were being faxed to the National Planning Commission for some surreptitious activity. He provided some details and fingered the Deputy Director of Administration, Mr. ʿTayo Kuponiyi, as the perpetrator. I was surprised that 'Tayo would collaborate with my detractors at NISER. Incidentally, he was the one who welcomed me to

NEIC on my assumption of duty and had reminded me that I was his senior at the Comprehensive High School, Aiyetoro. It was he, who also introduced me to the Secretary of NEIC, General Garba Mohammed, putting in words for me about my competence.

I intimated the General of this betrayal and he immediately contacted Mr. Fatoki directing that copies of the said documents be made available to him. After he had confirmed that the documents were authentic and that my account of the event was correct, he invited 'Tayo Kuponiyi who owned up to this fact. The General openly expressed his disappointment and lamented that he had put too much trust in 'Tayo allowing him unfeterred access not only to his office but to ALL documents that were under lock and key.

I was palpably disturbed by this revelation because the enemy was not just at the door step but was now within. As I returned home from work I knelt down and prayed using Psalm 35. The next day a meeting of the full NEIC committee was held. The committee adjudged that the appropriate punishment for the breach was dismissal but all things considered, 'Tayo was immediately redeployed away from the Presidency after due consultation with the SGF.

The Director-General was soon to receive another shock. On the directive of the new SGF, his action on my purported retirement was declared a nullity. He came personally to see the SGF and those who were in attendance reported that he pleaded with the SGF on the embarrassment which a reversal of his decision would cause him while reminding the SGF of the good times they spent together when they were both in the administration of the National Institute for Policy and Strategic Studies (NIPSS). The SGF thereafter directed that the matter be put in the cooler. Soon afterwards, Alhaji Gidado Idris passed on and it turned out anyway, that it was not a matter for the Office of the SGF but rather the Office of the Head of Service (OHOS)

NISER made a tactical error in its reply to a most damaging petition I sent to the Governing Council, by writing the Office of the SGF and copying the Office of the Head of the Civil Service instead of the reverse. The four Yoruba officers among them, the Permanent Secretary General Services Office (GSO) who handled the case in the Office of the SGF appeared, *ab initio*, to have compromised the position of the SGF who asked for my comments on the letter from NISER. I understood the game fairly well. In Yoruba internecine wars, you are confronting forces and bonds which meet more than the eye. They are the forces/bonds that delineate antagonists and protagonists. After a stage-managed meeting on the NISER's correspondence, the OSGF forwarded its position to the OHOS. On receiving this letter, it was rumoured that it became a spectacle among the top hierarchy of the officers from the core North of what the Yorubas were writing about themselves. For reasons far beyond my comprehension, officers of the Middle-Belt and the Core North now took greater interest in the matter.

I made enquiries about the position of the OHOS on the copy of the letter by NISER and was gratified by their assessment. But the letter should now be treated along with the position of the OSGF. A number of senior officers from the core North stood up for me. This included at least one Permanent Secretary and beyond. This was in contrast to the supposed gang up by people of my own ethnic group in the OSGF. Frantic efforts by NISER to influence decision in this theatre of the operation was fruitless.

The Director of Administration, OHOS (Mallam Hassan Saleh), needed clarification on certain aspects of my written comments and invited me for a meeting. On my way to this very important meeting, I stopped to inform our new NEIC Secretary, Malam Ibrahim Zukogi, who instructed our Director of Administration and Finance, Malam Musa Saleh, to accompany me for support. The meeting went very well. The initiator merely found some of my claims so horrific that he needed some documentary evidence to back them up. Those documents, to his constellation, were readily available. The presence of Musa Saleh at the meeting lent credence to my presentation because, unknown to me, the two Salehs had been childhood friends.

Work was concluded in the OHOS and, in terms of procedure, the Office would now forward the file to the superintending ministry of NISER, which was the National Planning Commission, to give effect to its decision. On his receipt of the file, the Honourable Minister briefed and obtained the approval from the President. Thereafter, one early morning my intelligence networks in both Abuja and Ibadan informed me that the Director-General received a phone call that morning directing him to turn in his resignation letter before the close of day or be fired. In any case, a new Director-General would be announced on the 4 p.m. news broadcast. The directive to the NISER Director-General was complied with and by 4 p.m. there were thunderous cheers of triumph at NISER, Ibadan, where people had been awaiting the 4 p.m. news bulletin.

In the next few days, I received my copy of the letter directing NISER on my correct designation of Research Professor, my date of retirement and my length of service. The acting Director-General immediately complied with the directives of the Ministry. The detractors who had vowed I would never earn the title of Research Professor had been put to shame as had those who worked against "exposure" because in this latter case, the year before this incident, I had been appointed Director and Head of Mr. President's Policy Think Tank, the Independent Policy Group (IPG). Again, man proposed and God disposed!!!

At the inception of a new civilian administration in 1999, a number of international organizations namely, the Ford Foundation, the UNDP and George Soros jointly funded the Independent Policy Group (IPG) to assist Mr. President with independent and unbiased advice on all critical issues of public policy. The IPG was, therefore, to serve as Mr. President's Policy Think Tank. In order not to compromise its objectives, the IPG was not to be part of the civil/public service and was designed to interact with Mr. President in a relaxed mood and environment at his residence, not in the office. The IPG was also to have unfettered access to the President.

Professor Dotun Phillips, who had retired from NISER several years back, was invited to help establish the outfit. At the interview for a substantive Director of the IPG, Professor Bade Onimode, not Professor Dotun Phillips, emerged the preferred candidate. A few years later, however, Professor Bade Onimode developed a terminal illness and passed on. He was succeeded by Professor Mike Kwanashie who, after about a year on the saddle, was appointed by Mr. President as Adviser for Social and Economic Affairs. Professor Kwanashie informed me of the vacancy and secretly hoped I would show interest. My own investigation showed that Professor 'Demola Oyejide of the University of Ibadan was the preferred candidate of the Honourable Minister of Finance, Dr. Okonjo Iweala and the Governor of the Central Bank, Professor Charles Soludo as well as some Senior Professors of the Department of Economics, University of Ibadan. Professor Oyejide had been interviewed by the President and was found appointable. Against this background, I decided not to show interest. However, the IPG was expressing frustration at its new appointee because of his inability to stay on the job. Apparently there had been some misinformation about Professor 'Demola Oyejide's availability. The IPG was therefore shopping again for a Director. I was not oblivious of this development. However, out of intuition, I was reluctant to declare interest in the job even though Professor Kwanashie considered me a better candidate.

In January 2004, while on one of my regular visits to Ibadan, I decided to visit the famed coffee-room of the Faculty of Social Sciences, University of Ibadan, but mindful of the interaction on public policy that takes place there, I said a short prayer for God's guidance on whatever interaction might involve me. At the Faculty, the first man I ran into was Professor Oyejide. He immediately approached me and briefed me of his situation with IPG and urged me to show interest in the position. I indicated that I would be willing to consider it. I informed Professor Mike Kwanashie of the encounter and then confided in him that, now that a controversy was not likely to develop over my candidacy, I was willing to be considered for the position. He immediately offered to send someone to collect my updated *curriculum vitae* (CV). But considering his unrelenting effort and our long-term relationship, I offered to bring it personally if he promised me a cup of coffee. He promised and I kept my word.

It was a Friday morning when I submitted the CV. It was handed over to Dr. Olatunji Kolapo who had recently been appointed Nigeria's High Commissioner to Ghana. The Ambassador intended to book an appointment for me to see the President on Monday night but I requested for Tuesday since I was to spend that weekend visiting my wife who was on admission at the University College Hospital, Ibadan. On Tuesday, at 8 p.m. I met with Mr. President who was in shorts and a T-shirt in the Villa living-room. He perused my CV and told the ambassador to tell the donors I was acceptable to him. I was soon to find out that the President had actually turned down two other candidates the night before. These were Professor Femi Taiwo of the Department of Economics, University of Ilorin who was actually a personal candidate of the new Director-General of NISER, and Dr. Kayode Adegbola Familoni, who was Head of the Department of Economics, University of Lagos. I met the donors two days after. The meeting was chaired by Ambassador Donald McHenry who had replaced Mr. Andrew Young as the United States Ambassador to the United Nations. He was particularly impressed by my association with Claremont Graduate School (CGS) and reminisced over contributions that graduates of CGS had made to the policy conceptualization in the Presidency of the United States.

I assumed duty in IPG on 18th March, 2004, and worked through the President's second term. In deciding how to interact with Mr. President, the IPG under my headship set out some guidelines. The most important was against the background that Mr. President's access to information and advice was almost limitless. Therefore, unless our contribution to knowledge was critically assessed to be new, we would not seek audience with him. Additionally, since our meeting with Mr. President could be at his instance, we identified a number of experts in various fields who could enrich our knowledge on a subject matter of interest at an in-house seminar or, who might if the need arose, accompany us to meet Mr. President. Discussions with Mr. President were of course privileged, and therefore strictly confidential. He met with my team 29 times for an average of one and a half hours for each meeting. The reports of the interactions have since been declassified and are available in the Presidential Library in Abeokuta.

At the conclusion of my stay with the IPG, I thought it would be most meaningful if I went into teaching to impart my knowledge and experience to the younger generation. I therefore applied to Bowen University, Iwo, Nigeria for a teaching appointment.

Even though I interviewed well, I did not get feedback from Bowen University for months. In the first week of September 2007, I met the General Secretary of the Nigerian Baptist Convention, Dr. Ademola Ishola, who incidentally was also the Visitor of the University, at the instance of Dr. Peter Oyedemi who was at the time, the Reverend at the Love Baptist Church, Akobo Ojurin, Ibadan. I intimated to the General Secretary whom I had met a few times when he was our Guest Preacher at the Aso Villa Chapel in the Presidential Villa, Abuja, that the University was reluctant to engage me because I was presumed to be a politician in view of my long association with Governments at both the federal and state levels. I further explained to him that if the University was concerned about my association with the Government, it would be even more concerned if it knew that I was a traditional ruler. He asked a few questions about my family life and browsed through my CV. He assessed me to be the kind of resource material which the University should seek to attract. In the United States, he remarked, quite a number of Universities would be interested in my service. We met on a Friday and by Monday morning he had arranged an appointment for me with the Vice Chancellor (Professor Timothy O. Olagbemiro). The Vice Chancellor was still unsure whether he wanted me. He explained that he already had three Professors in the Economics Department so, if engaged, I would be the fourth. He nevertheless directed that I see the Pro-Chancellor, Deacon Professor Bisi Sobowale. The Pro-Chancellor also browsed through my CV, confirmed that I had seen the General Secretary and Visitor of the University, then gave his approval. I assumed duty in Bowen on 10th September, 2007.

There were still a few indications that I was not welcomed in Bowen University. There were no professors on ground in the Department of Economics, contrary to what had been claimed by the Vice Chancellor. Also, I was allocated the same office space (a 10x12 feet room) with four other lecturers. However, since I was the most senior in the Department, I was later made the Head. In this position, I faced quite a number of challenges, especially during the conduct of and grading of examinations as well as during the processing of results. There were also some unusual encounters with students of the opposite sex. Young as they were, they would indulge in uncommon familiarity and discussions. Upon inquiry, I was informed that this was at the instance of Management, a strategy adopted by the administration to identify lecturers who might prey on the students. But for these nuisances, Bowen provided a very conducive environment for achieving my objective of imparting my experience and knowledge to the next generation of leadership in the country.

Even though I had intended for my stay at Bowen to be brief, I was there for eleven years. I served not only as Head of Department, but also as Dean of the Faculty of Social and Management Sciences, Member of the University Council and Director of the Entrepreneurship Centre. I was deeply gratified that very many of my students considered me a role model, asking me on several occasions, how they could be like me! The Deanship was of particular interest to me. In my final year at the Baptist Academy in Lagos, two of my colleagues and I had engaged in a discussion on our ambition in life. One had expressed the hope of becoming the Chief of the Army, the other, the Prime Minister and I, the Dean of the relevant Faculty in a University. Here I was becoming Dean even after I had occupied several positions higher than the Deanship.

The University had tremendous potentials except that it might have imbibed the endemic Nigerian malaise of insisting on preponderance of its staff, especially the leadership, coming from a dominant clan. At the end of the eleventh year, I voluntarily allowed my contract appointment to run out while appreciating the University Council for granting me the opportunity to serve at Bowen. Three Professors were particularly critical to the success and reputation of the University. They were Professors J. A. Faniran, Moses Oyeleke Fawole and D.S. Izebvaye. I hope that posterity will adequately recognize their invaluable contributions to the development, discipline and quality standard of the University. Their early disengagement was ominous and had wide ranging implications for the development of the institution.

Policy Think Tank

IPG Dinner With President Olusegun Obasanjo

Bowen

With Select Members Of Bowen University Council & Administrators

With Prof. Imoagene (L) & Prof. Izevbaye at Bowen

CHAPTER 8

BEWARE WHAT YOU WISH FOR YOURSELF

In 1951, my father decided to spend his annual leave with his brother (Ogunleye) in Aba, in the Eastern Region of Nigeria. During the leave in Aba, both brothers decided to take a road trip to Lagos with a stopover in Isotun, which my father would be visiting for the first time. At Ifon (now in Ondo State), their brand-new car broke down and the spare part required could only be bought in Lagos. The senior brother went to purchase the spare part while my father waited in the car. My uncle who was an elephant hunter knew that their car had broken down in elephant territory and had, with help of some farmers in the neighbouring town, secured the car with a number of totem poles. The trip to Lagos and back took 2 days during which my father reported several sightings of herds of elephants, crossing the road.

The trip to Isotun took place nevertheless and was the second most topical of their report of the trip, besides the breakdown of the car and the herds of elephants. From the moment the story of Isotun was told, my cousins and I developed very keen interest in visiting. However, for decades after, our parents would not take us home for the fear of losing us to some witch or wizard.

In January of 1964, I resumed for the Higher High School Certificate course at the Comprehensive High School, Aiyetoro, and met quite a number of students of Ijesa origin who had never been home. Together, we established the Ijesa Students Union and our first objective was an excursion to Ijesland. Segun Olowofoyeku, whose father was a Minister in the Western Regional Government, was going to be our host. Unfortunately, the political crisis in the Western Region had taken a turn for the worse by the time of our scheduled trip. The trip was then considered by the union to be unsafe and was aborted. However, I struck a bargain with Segun Olowofoyeku to be his only guest. Meanwhile, I had intimated my father of the planned trip and had requested of him the direction to Isotun. He replied promptly providing the direction but reiterating his concern for my safety. However, he said he took solace from the fact that I was going under the auspices of a student's union.

On the appointed day, we proceeded first to Ibadan and stayed two nights with Segun's family. On the third day his father arranged for us to set out for Ilesa. He provided us with a car and an armed security detail. Segun Olowofoyeku and I paid a short visit to my cousin, Mabel Iyabo James (now Mabel Iyabo Sanomi), who had been closely monitoring my adventure, to brief her of my movement. She was at the time a pupil midwife at the Adeoyo State Hospital, Ibadan. We departed on schedule and spent the night at the Olowofoyeku's residence at Oke Imo, Ilesa. On the following morning we rented two bicycles for which we eventually paid nine schillings each, and departed for Isotun.

The description to Isotun by my father required that we turn off to the left from the main road at Ibodi. However, we were approaching from Ilesa and soon after we got past the present site of the High Court of Justice, at Arimoro, we saw a signboard directing us to Isotun. We followed that direction through to

Isotun but there was now some confusion. My father had said the Family House was the first to the left. Now it would have to be the last to the right. As we approached the last house to the right, people began to congregate in front of the second to the last house. We descended from our bicycles and walked to the gathering. I prostrated to greet them and introduced myself (just like my father had advised) as "Omo Baba Eko". i.e. son of the father in Lagos. They replied almost instantly that they knew! Then I asked as directed by my dad, to see Pa Fapohunda and they replied that they had sent for him. In less than a minute, "Pa Fapohunda" appeared. I later learnt that the Pa Fapohunda had actually passed on but that Pa Lawrence was filling in. He received me familiarly, invited me into the house, ordered for palm wine, and directed that a goat be slaughtered and pounded yam prepared. Yet, Segun Olowofoyeku and I were not sure we were in the right place. However, as soon as the supposed "Pa Fapohunda" stepped out of the living-room, Segun Olowofoyeku said to me: "you look exactly like this man" to which I added " this man looks exactly like my dad ". We looked around in the living-room and found hanging on an Almanac, a picture of my Aba uncle with all of his children including Iyabo whom we had gone to bid goodbye before our departure from Ibadan to Ilesa. Now, we were sure our mission had been accomplished.

One remarkable event then took place. I was conducted on a tour of the three family houses and on the pavement of one of them was written, "Omo Owosekun". I asked questions about this name which questions elicited virtually the whole family history. It turned out that my grandfather's family name was "Owosekun" which had been the subject of research for my father and his brothers in Lagos. Several family meetings to which I accompanied my father at Andrews Street, Lagos

Island, were held on this matter. The family in Lagos had wanted to revert to the family name but it had no information on exactly what it was. The name "James" which their father had bequeathed to them was beginning to be embarrassing because many people were associating it with returnee-slaves. Having been satisfied with the family history that was told, I informed my father immediately upon my return to Lagos and changed my own last name to "Owosekun". My brothers, sisters and cousins followed suit. On the conclusion of the tour of the family houses we went to Ilesa township to know the family house at Araromi near the Atakunmosa Market.

I returned to Lagos the following day with different kinds of fruits, but it was the Cocoa Pod which generated the greatest sensation. None of my siblings and cousins had seen one before. Two years later, I left for the United States but visited Isotun again in 1974 in the company of my father.

In 1980, I was informed that the reigning monarch of Isotun had gone to join our ancestors and that it was the turn of our family to produce the successor. I reasoned that God had endowed me with all I needed in life and that I should therefore not show interest in spite of the seemingly genuine preference for my candidacy. The pressure continued for seven years following which I entered into an agreement with the elders of the family to ascend the throne. The conditions which I stipulated, and to which they agreed, were essentially three: a) that I would not be pressurized to take another wife, b) that I would not be required to be a member of any secret society, and c) that I would not be required to quit my job which meant that the Council of Chief/Elders would play a very prominent role in my reign. On my part, I was persuaded by the argument that our lineage last ascended the throne in 1874 and that we might lose our claim to the throne because when in 1946 it was our turn to mount the saddle, we were unable to produce a suitable candidate. If this trend continued, it was argued, we might lose our claim to the throne. I reached an agreement with the Elders in September of 1987 and by December of the same year, my most junior uncle (Chief J.O. James) declared his candidacy arguing it was the turn of his generation. He was invited for a meeting by the elders following which he personally informed me that he had withdrawn from the race and would be available to give me support for the throne. He kept his promise to the letter. But a cousin who had been Chairman of the meeting of members of the family in Lagos thereafter quickly expressed interest but when requested to show up to openly declare his interest, he declined to do so.

The first assignment for the family was to ensure acceptability of its nominee by the community. Therefore, on the appointed date, all members of the family in Lagos, Ibadan and Ilesa were required to assemble at the family House at Okero. At some point when I thought the family was running behind time, I suggested that I be allowed to proceed ahead of the others. However, I was advised not to, because beginning from the day I was introduced to the community till my installation, I had to enter the community by a special route which they were yet to show me. We all eventually set out in a convoy and lo and behold, we took that alternate route which Segun Olowofoyeku and I had taken during my first visit to Isotun in 1964. The Most Glorious Apostolic Church Divine Atundaolu, was the chosen venue for the introduction over the Local Authority School for reason of logistics. I was warmly received, and my candidacy was approved by the community. All other traditional requirements and rites were to be initiated by the family and community as the case might be, and in a weeklong ceremony beginning from the 9th of April, 1988, I was installed as the Asotun of Isotun.

On the night of 9th April, at about 11 p.m, my mom, my maternal uncle and I were seated round the table in the open air when my uncle expressed surprise at the day's event. In expressing his shock, he reminded us of the fact that he and my father of blessed memory, were very good friends and often patronized a social club at Campus Square, Lagos. He reported that on some rare occasions my dad would rise from his seat, lifting up his shirt and drawing attention to the rare mark on his belly and asserting that he was a prince and that if he did not become a king, one of his sons would. My uncle was deeply gratified that he was alive to witness the fulfilment of that prophesy which at that time they considered a joke.

On at least one occasion between 1995 and 2000, I visited the Paramount Ruler of Ijesaland (Owa Obokun) in the company of my uncle to explain to him that we had evidence in our ancestral home and from other sources that the status of the Asotun of Isotun is that of a Recognised Oba having been so gazetted in 1957 and a Chieftaincy declaration published in that regard in 1960. This Chieftaincy declaration was in the same 1960 compendium in which the declaration of the Paramount ruler was published. We explained to him that we were therefore seeking his cooperation to get the record corrected. He dismissed our explanation and directed that the matter not be raised with him again for consideration. Following this unfortunate encounter, I contacted a trusted friend with connections in Government who helped me with contacts in the relevant state government ministry.

After several months of futile effort, however, I was advised to seek a court declaration. I engaged the services of a lawyer who further made enquiries specially to confirm that the 1976 review of the Chiefs Law did not adversely affect my recognition. At the same time that I was taking these steps, I received the copy of a letter written by the Chairman, Atakunmosa West Local Government and addressed to the State Government drawing attention to the omission of some recognized Obas namely, the Asotun of Isotun, the Olosu of Osu, and Alagunmodi of Itagunmodi and two others, in public records and advising that the error be rectified. As this advice fell on deaf ears, three of us, the Olosu of Osu, the Alagunmodi of Itagunmodi and I, consulted on the matter and agreed that we would challenge the stance of the Government in court by seeking a declaration.

On the day that the case was opened in court, we were visited, while still in court, by the secretary to the Paramount Ruler who delivered a message inviting us to meet the Paramount Ruler immediately after the court hearing. Two of us honoured the invitation. The Paramount Ruler was visibly upset and as we explained that it had nothing to do with him since he was not even a plaintiff or defendant, he stood up and walked out on us while threatening that we should withdraw the case or else! We dared him and continued with the case nevertheless. I was personally aggrieved by his blatant disrespect to us and for his total disregard for the inalienable right of the communities we represented.

Our case was in the State High Court but I had expressed my concern to our lawyer that the judge might not have the effrontery to deliver judgment against his employer. I had therefore admonished the lawyer to prepare grounds for appeal if push came to shove. Expectedly, the judgment was not definitive. While we had shown evidence that the State Government was reluctant to take up the matter, the judgment was requiring us to enter into discussion with the defendant. We proceeded to file an appeal at the Appeals Court in Ibadan. After a few appearances at the Appeal Court, we were approached by the state counsel who suggested an out-of-court settlement. We agreed after some assurances that the settlement would be treated with due diligence. In the final resolution of the matter, I received from Government the following: a letter dated 5th April 2005 which read in part:

"I am directed to refer to your representation dated 14th September, 2004, and to inform you that after in-depth investigations, it has been pellucidly established that your Chieftaincy was inadvertently omitted from the list of Recognised... Chieftaincy... of Osun State 2001.

In the circumstances, the Executive Council of Osun State at its meeting of Wednesday, 9th March, 2005, has approved that your Chieftaincy be restored to the list of recognized chieftaincies... with effect from the time of inadvertent omission."

One of the most gratifying aspects of the resolution is the agreement by government that our status as Recognised Obas was acknowledged without any loss in continuity. Arrangements were now being made to present the Staff of Office to each of the plaintiffs. This presentation was to be made by the Executive Governor himself and was to have been made effective at the time of my installation seventeen years earlier.

It is important to note that as soon as the process for out-of-court negotiations commenced, the Paramount Ruler wrote four different petitions to Government outrightly opposing our negotiating positions. He even went to court to restrain the Executive Governor from presenting the Staff of Office. The court relief was filed by the Paramount Ruler in case HIL/94/05 in the High Court of Justice, Osun State of Nigeria, Ilesa Division on 4th November, 2005, and signed by Lai Babatope, Esq. However, the date for the hearing of the suit on the restraining order turned out to be a public holiday.

In its reply to the several petitions of the Paramount Ruler, the State Government not only conveyed its approval of my restoration but further clarified the limitations of the powers of the traditional ruler. A letter dated 15th August 2005 and referenced CD.7/1/Vol.9/529 read in part: "Only the

State Government can determine which Chieftaincies were inadvertently omitted from the list of recognized Chieftaincies being the custodian of the laws of the State."

The opposition of the Paramount Ruler was not limited to written petitions and seeking interim injunction. At the State Executive Council meeting he insisted, through emissaries who were already members of the Council, that my title be prefixed by "looja" which prefix he had described as "Village Head" in his book "The Head That Wears The Crown". The prefix had no effect on the Council's approval and in due course, I petitioned and was allowed to revert to the correct title of Asotun of Isotun. I have it on authority that on the eve of the presentation of the Staff of Office, the Paramount Ruler personally pleaded unsuccessfully with the Executive Governor, in a telephone conversation, not to go to Isotun the following day.

Our triumph was to have tremendous impact on the traditional rulership in Ijesaland. Hitherto, the Paramount Ruler forbade other Recognised Obas who were direct descendants of Oduduwa from displaying or carrying any paraphernalia of office, not even a walking stick or horse tail. Additionally, you were to prostrate before him and to appear before him without wearing any shoe or cap. Yes!!! This was true even for those whose status of Recognised Obas was nowhere disputed. This presentation of Staff of Office would put an end to that. The Paramount Ruler confided in a close associate of mine that his opposition to my correct status derived from the expectation that the presentation of the Staff of Office would open the floodgate for all other Recognised Obas.

The presentation of the Staff of Office took place seamlessly and it was followed by "endless" applications to the Governor by other recognised Obas who had been denied the privilege to receive the Staff of Office since their installations. I was reliably informed that during a sympathy visit to the Paramount Ruler, on the occasion of the fire incident in his palace, he disparaged the presentation of Staff of Office to so many recognised Obas. He was reported to have said that the recipients would all have very good use for their "staff" in "Irokoja". Irokoja is the traditional expansive palace ground of the Owa Obokun where crop production and animal husbandry take place. This aspersion is very often revisited in the circle of Obas till this day, with the remark that the aspersion applied not just to some of those who had recently been honored but to all who lay claim to a Staff of Office in Ijesaland.

In view of our experience with the Paramount Ruler on our recognition and several other matters of concern to traditional rulership in Ijesaland, especially the determination and disbursement of stipend, my colleagues and I considered our job unfinished. We felt that in the interest of Ijesaland, and in order to reduce rancor and acrimony, there was the need to create a separate Traditional Council for Atakunmosa East and Atakunmosa West Local Government Areas, to be called Ijesa South Traditional Council while what was left of the old Ijesa Traditional Council to which we now belonged as of right, be called Ijesa Central Traditional Council with the Paramount Ruler as Chairman. We initiated the move by visiting and obtaining support of three leading Traditional Rulers namely, the Ogboni of Ipole, the Awara of Iwara and the Adimula of Ifewara. My colleagues, the Awara, Olosu, and Alagunmodi, gave me the privilege of preparing the draft document for the new Council which document was approved by the Government a few years thereafter.

In Osun State, all Recognized Obas, whether Paramount, Consenting, Beaded or Non-Beaded, are referred to as Part II Obas which is a synonym for "Recognised Obaship". This does not mean that there are no hierarchical structures. The chief's law is in two volumes referred to as Part I and Part II.

While Part I is the preamble, the Recognized Obas are listed in Part II along with their respective domains. Therefore, in Yorubaland generally, and in Osun State in particular, there are two broad categories of Recognised Traditional Rulers. These are the Beaded and the Non-Beaded. The Beaded are in three sub-categories: those who have a history of ruling over an empire and are consenting authorities and/or are spiritual rallying point over a broadly defined geographical area linked by ancestry. The word "consent " is the process of referral by the Government to the Paramount Ruler to ensure a peaceful and smooth transition of rulership which succession is devoid of ascendancy by an impostor to the throne. The referral by government for consent takes place after a vacancy has been conveyed by the King Makers to the Local and State Governments and a selection process has been concluded at the community level with the assistance of the Local and State Governments. The referral to the Paramount Ruler is only part of the process and it is not open-ended. The response is time bound—only fourteen days, failing which Government may proceed as it deems fit. The second sub-category of Beaded Crown Obas comprises those who, though are consenting authorities, have no imperial history but may constitute a spiritual rallying point, while the third sub-category is of those who have neither imperial background nor consenting authority, nor are they spiritual rallying points.

After the presentation of the Staff of Office to me in Isotun, the Executive Governor proceeded to Itagunmodi and lastly to Osu. So, by providence, I became the first direct descendant of Oduduwa in Ijesaland, other than the Paramount Ruler, to be presented with a Staff of Office. Additionally, I was the first Professor to be installed a Recognized Oba in all Yorubaland. On this assertion, my attention has been drawn to the case of Professor Afolayan of the Obafemi Awolowo University (OAU), now deceased, who in the 1980s ascended the throne of Akesin of Ora Igbomina but his title was not sustained in the court. I decided not to seek for the beaded crown for the stool of the Asotun not only because of the cost of doing so but also because of the mammoth effort that might be associated with it especially the contact with the Paramount Ruler. However, a few years after the presentation of the Staff of Office, the Government approved a beaded crown for the Olosu of Osu and pressure began to mount on me because, historically, Isotun was more ancestral than Osu. His Royal Majesty, the Awara of Iwara, was the first to give me encouragement. He promised to provide every possible assistance and he fulfilled this promise far beyond expectation. I must confess that till this day, I do not know what endeared me so much to the Awara, His Royal Majesty Oba Adewale Kassim.

A major development followed the approval of the beaded crown to the Olosu. It became settled in law that the power to approve beaded crown for Traditional Rulers is vested in the Governor, not the Paramount Ruler. Now my application would go not to the Paramount Ruler but to the Governor who would seek the advice of the Osun State Council of Obas and approval of the State Executive Council which he chaired. Oba Awara ensured that the Governor received my application and minuted on it to the Osun State Council of Obas where incidentally the Paramount Ruler is Deputy Chairman and his opposition would be fatal.

Preparatory to the meeting of the Council of Obas, Oba Awara had arranged with some prominent individuals to help us soften the ground with His Imperial Majesty Oba Okunade Sijuade, Olubuse II, the Ooni of Ife who was the Chairman of the Council. However, there was a disappointment and the individuals were not able to provide the assistance they had so confidently promised, citing that it might jeopardize their personal relationship with the Paramount Ruler. Oba Awara then suggested he and I see the Ooni but this plan also fell through, following which I obtained from him the personal phone number of the Ooni and booked an appointment to see him. My appointment was for the 31st of March, against a meeting that was scheduled for the following day. The Ooni was pleased to receive me. He called me simply " Professor" and inquired to know my mission. Unfortunately, he most recently developed difficulty with his hearing and we needed to call in one of his "emeses", to repeat my communication loudly so he could hear me well. He requested to peruse my application which incidentally I was not carrying on me. I assured him that it would be placed before him at the meeting. He reminded me that "the meeting is tomorrow" to which I answered in the affirmative. There was not much more conversation we could have because of our communication problem.

I opened my briefing with Oba Awara by saying "if we get approval for this application, it would be God's doing." I explained that if Ooni had lost his hearing how was he to remember my request at the meeting of the State Council of Obas? On returning home in Ibadan, Olori was anxious to be briefed and I repeated what I had told Oba Awara and we both left it to God. The following day, I received a congratulatory phone message from Oba Awara. The Paramount Ruler, who would have most certainly opposed my application, was absent from the meeting. On 2nd June, 2010, the Osun State Executive Council approved Beaded Crowns for the Asotun of Isotun and three other Obas in Osun State. I was on the way from my teaching assignment at Bowen University when the news broke. I proceeded directly to my church where they were holding the weekly prayer meeting, walked up to the pulpit, knelt down and gave thanks. The Pastor, who officiated the prayer-meeting, called me later in the fear that I might have been befallen by a major calamity. I assured him that, on the contrary, all was well.

The coronation ceremony took place on 30th August, 2010, with the Governor and several dignitaries in attendance. When asked why he would not accompany the Governor to the event, the Paramount Ruler was reported to have replied that he was not invited by the Asotun. That was true. He was not invited. It is worthy to note that seven years later, someone obliged me with a copy of the petition which the Paramount Ruler had written against the decision of the Osun State Council of Obas to approve my application for a Beaded Crown. The petition was dated 26th April, 2010, and addressed to the Chairman, Osun State Council of Obas. I was seeing the petition seven years after God had declared it a nullity!!! When GOD is with us WHO can be against Us!!!

Kingship

With Governor Olagunsoye Oyinilola At The Coronation

With Olori At The Coronation

With Cheif L A Sofenwa My
Vice Principal At Aiyetoro

CHAPTER 9

EPIC BATTLE OVER OTA-IDE

It is important to keep in mind that until 2005, when I regained my status as a Recognised Oba without loss of continuity, I was considered a Minor Chief which status required that I defer to the Paramount Ruler in virtually all matters of tradition. The historical incident which I am about to recount should be viewed against this background.

A few days after my installation as Asotun of Isotun, the Elders of the community requested for an audience with me. They intimated to me that our ancestral home was rooted in Ota-ide on the Ijesa-Ede border and that we had lost control over it during the reign of my immediate predecessor (1946-1980). They pleaded with me to re-establish control over it as a matter of priority. Even though I understood their nostalgic feeling, I was very skeptical of their motive.

However, in December, 1988, the year of my installation, I sent two emissaries comprising Mr. Adeyemi Owosekun, the Ejemo of Isotun and Mr. Famoriyo Ikotun, who had been an Osomolo in Ota-ide, to inquire about the status of Ota-ide. They reported on the demise of Alakoso Abegunrin but were not able to meet his successor.

On the 29th April, 1989, the Asaobi honored my invitation to the first anniversary of my Installation which was marked with the award of a chieftaincy title of Yeye Jemo. There was a large gathering of Chiefs and well-wishers at the ceremony. On this occasion the Asaobi intimated to me, that his forefathers and mine were close friends and that they were neighbours in Ota-ide. He promised to show me the boundary between our two farmlands in Ota-ide if I would reciprocate his kind gesture. He later confided in me that the reciprocity he was referring to was my assistance with the Paramount Ruler for a Beaded Crown. At this time, it was erroneously believed that the authority to wear a beaded crown was the exclusive preserve of the Paramount Ruler. I gave him, the Asaobi, my word to the extent that the Paramount Ruler might accommodate such a request from me.

In a letter dated 10th July, 1993, and delivered by three emissaries to Mr. Ojo Abegunrin who was the son of the late Alakoso of Ota-ide, I introduced myself to the tenants at Ota-ide and requested for a re-establishment of Asotun's long standing relationship with them. This letter was incidentally collected from Ojo Abegunrin by the Asaobi who sat on it for several months without consulting with me.

On the 5th of January, 1994, I visited the Asaobi in his Ilesa residence in the company of Mr. Raphael Idowu Owosekun and Elder P. A. Badejo to inform him of my findings and my readiness to take possession of the Ota-Ide farmland. I requested for his assistance in identifying the boundary between our two farmlands. He instantly denied our encounter of 29th April, 1989, but advised that I seek help elsewhere. We agreed to exchange notes as I progressed with the investigation.

On 30th April, 1994, I held a meeting with Heads of all of the fifteen settlements which had been identified as those traditionally under the control of the Asotun in Ota-Ide. I attended the meeting in the company of Chief Adeyemi Owosekun, the Ejemo of Isotun, Elder P. A. Badejo, Chief Poju

Famoriyo Ikotun, the Saloro of Isotun, Mr. Raphael Idowu Owosekun and Mr. Lasisi Kasunmu, the Loriomo of Isotun. We were very well entertained and were presented with gifts of hot drink and money. As to the purpose of our mission i.e. re-establish of our control over the farmland, the tenants promised to consult with their elders in both Modakeke and Ede and revert to us.

In my letter of 12th May, 1994, I informed the Asaobi of our findings at Ota-ide providing details of the settlements under my control. I further intimated to him that the tenants on the farmland had been instructed to stop paying isakole (tax) to him henceforth. On the 14th of May, 1994, I received an invitation to see the Paramount Ruler at 10.00 a.m. on the 17th of May, 1994, at which meeting I was informed that the Asaobi had lodged complaints against me that:

a) I had addressed a letter to him whose content caused him grief, and

b) I had illegally occupied his traditional farmland.

However, the Asaobi did not show up at the meeting to personally make these accusations. Therefore, the accusations were neither formally made nor considered. The Asaobi also failed to show up on the rescheduled date of 4th June, 1994, following which I formally, in my letter of 6th June, requested the Paramount Ruler to, among other things, compel him to honour future invitations, and to set up a committee to investigate the claim and counter-claim of control over Ota-ide. In the interim, the Paramount Ruler sent one of his High Chiefs, the Bajemo, to confirm my claim especially, of an old palace building, an Agbe which is the symbol of the King's authority over life and death of his subjects, and an Akodi. In Ijesaland, the Agbe is particularly important as a necessary and sufficient condition for the status of Recognised Obaship. The confirmation by the

Bajemo was a game changer and an eye opener for me, about my Correct Status. It was an indisputable confirmation of the 1957 Regional Gazette publication that the Asotun of Isotun has always been a Recognised Oba.

On 26 August, 1994, when the Asaobi eventually showed up, I made an oral presentation in line with an advanced copy of the written deposition I had forwarded for the occasion. Following this deposition, the Paramount Ruler adopted my earlier request to set up a committee to investigate the veracity of my claim to the ownership of the Ota-Ide farmland. The committee was headed by the late Ogboni of Ipole and included the Olosu of Osu, the Saba of Ilesa, and the Lomofe of Ilesa as members. The committee, which was set up in September, was to complete its work no later than 12th October, 1994. However, because of the theatrics of the Asaobi the committee could not commence its work until the 19th of October. My witnesses and I deposed on the 26th and the Asaobi deposed on the 27th. Site inspection was also scheduled for the 27th October. My deposition on 26th October, 1994, is provided below:

DEPOSITION ON ISOTUN'S CLAIM OVER OTA-IDE

Location

Ota-Ide is located in Atakunmosa [West] Local Government Area of Osun State. It is about 10 km from Osu. The route via Osu, starting from the Police Station on the Iloba - Kajola road, is as follows:

a) Police Station to Akola [4km]

b) Akola to Asaobi's Residence [3km] and

c) Asaobi's Residence to Alusekere/Atagbado Ojo junction [3km]

Starting from the Alusekere/Atagbado Ojo junction on the Akola - Ede Road, Ota-Ide stretches North past Alusekere to the Shasha River which constitutes the boundary with Owa Obokun's farmland. It also stretches

South from this same junction terminating by the boundary with Iwaro Chieftaincy Farmland. Ota-Ide is again bounded on the West by the Shasha River. The whole of Ota-Ide is traversed by the Akola-Ede Road.

In summary, Ota-Ide is bounded on the North by the Shasha River [Owa Obokun's farmland] on the South by Iwaro Chieftaincy Farmland, on the West by the Shasha River, and on the East by Asaobi's farmland. A brief sketch of Ota- Ide is provided.

Crops

Annual Crops were predominant in Ota-Ide until the advent of cocoa. These annual crops included onions, yams, pepper, maize and beans. Now, however, perennial crops predominate. These include cocoa, kola nut, local palm fruits and oranges.

Origin of Isotun's claim

Atari-Agbo [olori agbo; Ewure [Obuko] o lori ati ba agbo kan] was installed the Asotun of Isotun by his uncle Owa Obokun, Obara Ale-tile, in 1823 over the territory now referred to as Ota-Ide. Atari-Agbo was succeeded as Asotun by his first son, Gbatoremu who reigned from 1852 to 1874. Gbatoremu's son, Olaiya Igbalajobi, later became the Aloya of Iloya. The third Asotun, Adegboro Owosekun, Owosekun I, who was Atari-Agbo's second son reigned from 1874 to 1916. Asotun Akinola Adeniyi Owosekun, Owosekun II, who is the incumbent Asotun, is a direct descendant of Atari-Agbo.

Evidence of Atari-Agbo's reign over Isotun [Ota-Ide] are the Apole [Ahoro], the Agbe, and the Court [Akodi]. Atari-Agbo unsuccessfully contested the Owaship against Owa Gbegbaje in 1832. The circumstances surrounding his unsuccessful bid led to Owa Gbegbaje granting Atari-Agbo extensive autonomy over the Ota-Ide domain. This explains the control of Atari-Agbo over an Agbe and Akodi. Indeed, there are two Apole sites in Ota-Ide. These are in respect of Isotun Oke and Isotun Isale/Odo.

Atari-Agbo lived in the latter. The former is close to the boundary with Asaobi's farmland. The site of the Apole of Isotun Oke is littered with Egudu holes.

Other sign posts in Ota-Ide include a huge Erinje tree which is now dead but whose offshoots [six] are still very visible. Also, there was an Iroko tree by the Church in Aba Abegunrin. However, only the stump of the Iroko tree now remains. In addition, the boundaries of Ota-Ide are, where necessary, marked with Peregun trees.

Atari-Agbo, between 1832 and 1852, moved to present day Isotun on the advice of the oracle in order to ensure the survival of his male children, several of whom he had already lost in rather mysterious circumstances. After the departure of Atari-Agbo for present day Isotun, Ota-Ide continued to be considered and treated as part of the Asotun's domain.

Asotun Adeyemi Jegede, the sixth Asotun, was the last Asotun to exercise effective control over Ota-Ide. On one of his several visits, Asotun Adeyemi Jegede went in the company of Adeyeye Daramola Adeniyi who later succeeded him as Asotun; Ige Agbefidu who was then the Saba of Isotun; Ale Adekankun whose son was later installed as Aro of Isotun; Eso Fapohunda Owosekun, the then Ejemo of Isotun; Adeyemi Owosekun who is currently the Ejemo of Isotun, and Raphael Idowu Owosekun. The reigning Asaobi [Oro] during this visit was the father of the current Asaobi [Abudu]. The party stayed in Ota-Ide for five days in the house of Alakoso Abegunrin and visited all the settlements in Ota-Ide. At the Agbe a porcupine attacked and injured Asotun Adeyemi Jegede. Asotun's party was escorted by the Alakoso Abegunrin and his son, Ojo, who is now the Balogun of Ajebandele.

Contact with Ota-Ide virtually ceased during the reign of Asotun Adeyeye Daramola Adeniyi who ascended the throne in 1946, after defeating Ige Agbefidu of the Owosekun Ruling House. He passed away in 1980. His neglect of Ota-Ide was largely due to the fact that he was so unpopular that after his installation in the Afin Adimula he was refused entry into present day Isotun. It took four months to settle the dispute with the citizenry. Even after this settlement, Asotun Daramola Adeniyi lived for the most part of his reign in Oke Padi in Ilesa and exercised very limited control over present day Isotun. A new Asotun was installed in April 1988, almost eight years after the passing away of Asotun Adeyeye Daramola Adeniyi. Therefore, for a span of 42 years there was virtually no contact with Ota-Ide except for a few but unsustained visits by the direct descendants of Atari-Agbo and frequent reports from an Isotun Indigene of the Alaka Ruling House, Mr. Famoriyo Ikotun, who worked in Ota-Ide as an Osomalo.

In December 1988, Asotun Owosekun II sent two emissaries comprising Adeyemi Owosekun, the Ejemo and Mr. Famoriyo Ikotun to Ota-Ide. They reported on the demise of Alakoso Abegunrin but could not meet with his "successor".

On 29th April, 1989, Asotun Owosekun II and Asaobi Abudu met in Isotun on the occasion of the installation of the Yeye-Jemo of Isotun. On this occasion, Asaobi Abudu intimated Asotun Owosekun II, in the presence of some Isotun chiefs and visitors, of the long-standing relationship between the Asotun and the Asaobi. As an example, he said that the Asotun's original traditional domain and the Asaobi's farmland are adjacent to one another near the boundary of Ede with Ijesaland. He broke kola, poured libation and prayed for the Asotun.

Visit of Asotun Owosekun II to Ota-Ide

On April 30, 1994, the incumbent Asotun paid a maiden visit to Ota-Ide. The meeting, which was held in Tokode, was attended by heads of all the settlements in Ota- Ide. The Asotun was accompanied by Adeyemi Owosekun, the Ejemo; 'Poju Ikotun, the Saloro; Lasisi Kasunmu, the Loriomo, Pa Raphael Idowu Owosekun and Elder P.A. Badejo. Asotun's party was entertained and in addition presents of hot drink and money were given to the Asotun.

Principal Tenants on Ota-Ide

There were a number of care-takers of Ota-Ide after Atari-Agbo's departure for present day Isotun. One Mr Abegunrin of Modakeke

99

Origin, and after whom one of the settlements in Ota-Ide is named, was the care-taker from about 1934 until his death in 1950. His son, Ojo Abegunrin, is currently the head of the family in Aba Abegunrin. Other notable tenants of Ota-Ide include Nasiru Babatapa who is a grandson of a Nupe hunter. The Nupe hunter had been allowed to settle in Ota-Ide by the Isotun indigenes. Also, one Mr. Fadeyi of Tonkere, near Alakowe, was once a tenant on the sites of both the Agbe and Ahoro or Apole where he found historical artifacts such as mortar and grinding stone. He was told that the artifacts belonged to the departed Isotun indigenes. The grinding stone is in the custody of Ojo Abegunrin.

Settlements in Ota-Ide and the respective Heads are detailed below:

S/NO	SETTLEMENT	HEAD OF SETTLEMENT
1.	Abegunrin	Mr. Ojo Abegunrin
2.	Amosun	Mr. Fatunbi
3.	Elegudu	Mr. Buraimoh
4.	Oke Ayogun	Mr. Yesufu Oke
5.	Tokode	Mr. Buraimoh Banji
6.	Aba Jide	Mr. Joseph Adeyemi Akinjide
7.	Aba Tapa	Mr. Nasiru Babatapa
8.	Ile Oke No. 1	Mr. Lamidi
9.	Ile Oke No. 2	Mr. Salami Adeagbo
10.	Aba Olode	Mr. Salau
11.	Alusekere	Mr. Jinadu
12.	Moteji	Mr. Oduola
13.	Aba Adekolu	Mr. Oke Adekolu
14.	Alabidun	Mr. Amusa Alagbe
15.	Aba Asunnara	Mr. Oloyede

The Conviction of Asaobi Abudu

As already noted above, Abudu is the son of Oro, the reigning Asaobi when Asotun Adeyemi Jegede visited Ota-Ide. On the death of Alakoso

Abegunrin in 1950, and before the funeral rites of Alakoso Abegunrin were concluded, Abudu attempted to alter the boundary between Ota-Ide and Asaobi's farmland. In the process he cut down about 60 cocoa trees.

Abegunrin's son [Ojo] who was still mourning his father's death was informed in Modakeke, of Abudu's encroachment. He reported the matter to Chief Loro Lajiga Falode, who advised him to bring the matter to the attention of Longe Faloyo, who was Asaobi's [oro's] neighbour and good friend. Both Chief Loro and Longe Faloyo invited Abudu and his father for a discussion in Chief Loro's compound. Abudu's father pleaded for leniency but his son, Abudu, was convicted and fined the sum of £80 [eighty pounds sterling] which he paid. Chief Loro and Longe Faloyo then obtained an assurance from Abudu that he [Abudu] would henceforth distance himself from Ota-Ide and would do no physical harm to Ojo Abegunrin. Abudu is the current Asaobi and he is reported to be collecting traditional rents [Isakole] on Ota-Ide.

Threats and Intimidation of Tenants by Asaobi Abudu

Asaobi Abudu has engaged in constant threat and intimidation of the tenants on Ota-Ide since the meeting of April 30, 1994 of the Asotun and the tenants. He has even threatened physical attack on some of the tenants if they persist in supporting the Asotun's claim. In consequence the tenants are reluctant to give evidence in the open.

There is therefore a need for the Panel to ensure adequate protection for tenants who may be willing to give evidence in order to encourage them to be credible.

Deposition Before Owa Obokun Aromolaran II

On August 26th, 1994 both the Asotun Owosekun II and Asaobi Abudu appeared before His Royal Majesty, Oba Gabriel Adekunle Aromolaran II, the Owa Obokun Adimula of Ijesaland on matters relating to this dispute. Three Chiefs namely, the Odole, the Segbua and the Bajemo were in attendance.

Two points are worthy of note in the deposition by Asaobi Abudu. Firstly, the Asaobi contended that the common boundary between the Asotun and the Asaobi which he intimated to the Asotun on 29th April 1989 was in respect of Isaobi and present day Isotun. However, two communities - Inisa and Okenasin - which currently constitute the domain of Loja Akesin, separate Isaobi from present day Isotun. Therefore, this aspect of the Asaobi's deposition lacks any basis in fact.

Secondly, the Asaobi, rather than respond directly to his conviction by Chief Loro Falode in 1950, referred to a court case over Ota-Ide in Ife.

Preliminary Ruling by Owa Obokun Aromolaran II

In his Preliminary ruling on August 26, 1994 His Royal Majesty, Oba Gabriel Adekunle Aromolaran II, restrained both parties from exercising any control over the disputed farmland until the final determination of the case.

Asaobi's violation of Owa's Restraining Order

In a blatant disregard for this ruling of His Royal Majesty, Oba Gabriel Adekunle Aromolaran II, the Owa Obokun Adimula of Ijesaland, the Asaobi:

a)   *Invited the tenants for a meeting;*

b)   *Informed them that the restraining order which was conveyed to them by Owa's Emese actually emanated from the Asotun not the Owa Adimula, and*

c)   *Demanded that the outstanding Isakole for 1994 be paid latest 15th October.*

Prayers

The Investigation Panel on the dispute over Ota-Ide is humbly invited to note that:

1. *Ota-Ide is located in Atakunmosa [West] local Government Area some 10 kms from Osu;*

2. *Ota-Ide devolved to Isotun following the installation of Atari-Agbo as the Asotun of Isotun by Owa Obokun Obara Ale-tile in 1823;*

3. *Contact between Isotun and Ota-Ide virtually ceased in the 34 years of the reign of the last Asotun and in the 8 years between his demise and the installation of the incumbent Asotun;*

4. *In the 42 years during which contact between Isotun and Ota-Ide was at its lowest ebb, the current Asaobi made two incursions into Ota-Ide:*

    i)   *While still under the tutelage of his father he was convicted of encroaching on Ota-Ide and was fined £80 [eighty pounds sterling] with an assurance that he would keep his distance from Ota-Ide and do no bodily harm to Ojo Abegunrin who is the son the late Alakoso;*

    ii) *In spite of the assurance given in 4, he is currently collecting Isakole on Ota-Ide.*

1. *On 26th August, 1994, His Royal Majesty Oba Gabriel Adekunle Aromolaran II, the Owa Obokun Adimula of Ijesaland, in his preliminary ruling restrained both parties from exercising any control over the disputed area until the final determination of the case.*

2. *The Asaobi has since violated this restraining order by inviting the tenants on the disputed area for a meeting, and by demanding that the Isakole for the balance of 1994 be paid latest by October 15.*

The Investigation Panel is humbly requested to uphold, having duly considered this deposition, the Asotun's claim over Ota-Ide.

There was an unusual drama at the site inspection. Before the commencement of the inspection, the Ogboni of Ipole, who was the chairman of the investigation committee, engaged in a long rhetorical to the effect that the Asotun should give up his claim to Ota-Ide because he (the Asotun) is not lacking in anything. I am thankful to all members of my team which included: Chief J. O. James, Mr. Raphael Idowu Owosekun, Mr. Adeyemi Owosekun, the Ejemo; Chief 'Poju Famoriyo Ikotun, the Saloro; Elder P.A. Badejo, Mr. Tunji Aluko, Mr. Okunade Aderibigbe Omirin and Mr. Lasisi Kasumu, the Loriomo, all of whom were unanimous that silence was the best answer to the theatrics. The inspection proceeded and all of our claims - old site of the Palace, Agbe, Akodi, erinje trees, the Peregun trees as demarcation of Asotun's farmland from Asaobi's farmland, and the Okuna (old footpath) as the demarcation of Asotun's farmland from Iwaro's farmland were shown to the committee.

There was another mild drama at the Agbe. The committee required both the Asaobi and I to swear in support of our claim of ownership. I explained to the committee that, except for the statutory requirement in a court of law, as a matter of principle, I do not swear. The Asaobi, on the other hand, eagerly took a handful of the soil from the Agbe and swore to the high heavens and ancestors, that he owned the farmland. This singular act is cited by many as the cause of the catalogue of calamities which befell the Asaobi beginning from the time immediately following the inspection.

The Chairman of the Committee received the draft copy of the Committee's report from the secretary and blatantly refused, for five months, to call a meeting of the Committee to consider it. I petitioned the Paramount Ruler and after the Chairman refused to carry out the Paramount Ruler's directive to consider the report, a new committee was set up. This second committee was chaired by High Chief Arapate.

On the completion of its assignment in early October 1995, the report was submitted to the Paramount Ruler at the statutory meeting of Ijesas held at the Oke Mese. The atmosphere at this meeting of Ijesa society was very tense as each chieftaincy category in Ijesaland commented on the report. The meeting was unanimous in its observation that the claim by the Asaobi was fundamentally flawed because, unlike the Asotun who is a Prince of Oduduwa, the Progenitor of the Yorubas, the Asaobi could not lay claim over a territory where an "Agbe" is located. Following this observation and other comments which were all in support of the Asotun's claim, the Paramount Ruler pronounced the Asotun the rightful owner of the Ota-Ide farmland.

Immediately after this judgement the Asaobi who was actually the custodian of one of the Paramount Ruler's deities, the Ijugbe, made an incendiary comment which provoked the Paramount Ruler to derobe him at this monthly meeting of the Ijesas. It was a most horrifying experience!!! The Paramount Ruler followed up with a letter to all heads of the settlements at Ota-ide directing them to recognise the Asotun as the rightful authority over Ota-ide.

Two months later, I was invited by the Paramount Ruler to a meeting at which he intimated to me that he had received several entreaties to pardon the Asaobi. I was surprised that he considered my view on the subject matter relevant because the pardon was entirely his prerogative. He explained that according to tradition, the Asaobi would join his ancestors if his chieftaincy title was not restored to him within three months. He subsequently pardoned the Asaobi. However, the unrelenting Asaobi immediately filed a case at the Okebode Customary Court against the Asotun. He was compelled to commence this case at the customary court level because, at that time, all land cases were required by law, to commence at the Customary court level.

The Customary Court at Okebode, where the case was filed, was presided over by the Aloya of Iloya, His Royal Highness, Oba

Ademiju assisted by Prince Agunlejika, and the Baale of Lala. I felt certain that Justice would be served at this court largely because the President, the Aloya of Iloya, was also the chairman of the Bilagbayo Ruling House (for the Paramount rulership of Ijesaland) to which I also belong. He is also reputed to be a custodian of Ijesa history. Prince Agunlejika, now of blessed memory, was also from the Bilagbayo Ruling House. My trust in this court was, however, misplaced.

The two judges were somewhat careless in their handling of the case. Many people had interceded on the side of the Asaobi and had elicited some assurances on what the judgment would be. I discretely made my own investigation and found out that the land in dispute was very well known to the judges and that their plan was to "make both of us happy" by dividing the farmland into two. I was greatly disappointed in the judges and immediately approached the High Court in Ilesa to disqualify the three judges and their court from further hearing the case. I was successful in this effort and at the venue where we all congregated for the site inspection, the Customary Court judges were served the Ruling of the High Court, following which I seized the initiative and filed a fresh case against the Asaobi at the Customary Court at Epe, which Court I had been reliably informed had a reputation for justice. The Court President was the Akire of Ikire Epe-Ijesa.

I was impressed with the court at Epe-Ijesa. It treated our case with dispatch and delivered judgement in my favor. The Asaobi remained unrelenting. The matter was, however, finally resolved in our favour at the High Court in Ilesa. Our rulership over Ota-Ide commenced from October 1995, immediately after the judgement of the Ijesas at the Oke Mese and I proceeded to rename the Farmland "Orile-Isotun."

The Yoruba tradition has always warned against engaging in a land dispute if you are not sure you are the rightful owner.

Given my Ota-Ide experience, I admonish the same. There were so many factors at play during the dispute over Ota-Ide. The Asaobi who was himself the Priest of "Ijugbe" deity elicited support from his personal priest who resided in Alabidun, which is situated on the disputed farmland, and from his peers in Iwo and Offa. Demons had a free reign. The Asaobi was accompanied to the site inspection by a number of his Chiefs and supporters with a lady carrying a pot of charms. Members of my own team were not left out. My uncle who was a proud high-ranking member of the Reformed Ogboni Fraternity (ROF), and some of my Chiefs would spend prolonged periods of time preparing for any of our outings on the dispute. Some of them would top this long preparation with one or more tots of alcohol. It was quite a spectacle. Fortunately, my mother had given me a strong Christian upbringing and I prayed and/or fasted as the situation demanded.

There were two schools of thought about me in my community. One was that I possessed superior demonic power, and the other held that I was the re-incarnation of Atari-Agbo who was displeased with the way his Kingdom was being managed and therefore returned to straighten things out. Rarely was there anyone who held a view that was different from these two. In the end, it was my God who prevailed.

While this dispute lasted, the Asaobi lost two of his children, he was involved in a near fatal accident, and eventually lost his life. He also suffered a lot of indignities. He was openly chided by his own Chiefs, at his traditional council meetings for attempting to steal Asotun's farmland. As earlier reported, he was dethroned and derobed. Also, in a face-saving effort at which he later (after the Court judgement) solicited the intervention of the Paramount Ruler, one of the two High Chiefs who were present on the occasion (which Chiefs included the Lejofi and the Arapate) openly chided the Asaobi in a manner and language that is unprintable, for contesting the authority of the Asotun of Isotun over Ota-Ide.

Even the supporters of the Asaobi were not spared. His chief priest a.k.a. Alamona, who resided on the Asotun's farmland set a trap for Mr. Okunade Aderibigbe Omirin and I to prevent the court-ordered sealing of his house. Unknown to us, he had mined the compound of his residence with charms which he intended would terminate our lives. The residents of Ota-Ide were witnesses to the fact that after the sealing of his house the priest lost two of his children on that same day. Alamona was eventually stricken with the fatal infection of necrotizing fasciitis (the flesh-eating bacterial infection) from which he eventually died. On his death-bed he was reported to have admonished his children never to involve themselves in any dispute about which they were not sufficiently knowledgeable.

In 2011, the successor to Asaobi Abudu, Asaobi Oluwagbemiga Emmanuel Olowe, made a desperate effort to reclaim Ota-Ide. He planted several signboards on the farmland claiming ownership. I reported the incident to the Police at Osu. Following the police investigation, Asaobi Olowe was given the option of a charge for contempt or an undertaking to the Police and the Asotun. He chose the latter.

Let me seize this opportunity to express my appreciation to all of those who stood by me during this dispute. They included Chief J. O. James, Chief Adeyemi Owosekun, Chief 'Poju Famoriyo Ikotun, Mr. Lasisi Kasunmu (now Mr. Lawrence Fayanju), Mr. Raphael Idowu Owosekun, Elder P. A. Badejo and Mr. 'Tunji Aluko. I am also very grateful for the invaluable support which I received from my nuclear family, and from Dr. (Now Professor) Vincent O. Akinyosoye and also from Prince (Now Loja of Kajola-Ijesa) Okunade Aderibigbe Omirin. There was nationwide scarcity of petroleum products during the entire period of the dispute. Professor Akinyosoye provided all the products that we needed. On his own part, Loja Omirin was always by my side. His understanding and experience of intrigues in Ijesa traditional politics helped to keep my strategies in focus.

CHAPTER 10

DEVELOPMENT EXPERIENCE

In the 1500's, Alaafin Sango commissioned the Agbalale Olofa Ina to set up a security post between Ara and Awo to protect the empire's trade routes to Apomu and Benin City. This security post was referred to as Ede-Ile. However, the Fulani invasion which affected Ejigbo through to Osogbo, caused the security post to relocate to present day Ede across the Osun River. The new Ede was established about 1817, by Timi Kubolaje Agbonran and his brothers: Oyefi, Ajenju, Arohanran and Oduniyi, most of whom took turns succeeding one another as Timi.

Incidentally, the new Ede laid between the Osun and Shasha Rivers. The latter river was the boundary between Ede and Ijesaland. The caravans passed the night at the trading post immediately across the Shasha River. This trading post was referred to as "Isotuntun" which was later shortened to "Isotun". The people of Isotun migrated, between 1832-1852, to present day "Isotun" and now call the ancestral home "Orile-Isotun." Orile is the farmland of the Asotun of Isotun. Therefore, Orile-Isotun cannot be left out of our development effort.

At my inauguration in April, 1988, infrastructural development was virtually none existent. Whether in Isotun or Orile-Isotun, there was no portable water, so people drank from streams; the road was not motorable most of the year; no health services were provided, though at Orile, there was a rickety health centre; school buildings were dilapidated and poorly staffed -- two teachers and sometimes one, to the primary school. No electricity. The churches, especially in Isotun, were in a sorry state of disrepair. This depicts a complete state of neglect, especially by government. The communities were on the verge of extinction. However, with the help of God, family, friends as well as well-wishers, Isotun has changed remarkably in the last thirty-five years.

There is now portable water which is provided from boreholes or deep wells. Thanks to communal effort, the roads are now motorable all year round. At Isotun, there is a modern health facility with provision for rural surgery-- hernia, lipoma, hydrocephalus and appendectomy. The Primary Health Care Centre was commissioned in 1998 and the first surgical procedures were performed under the direct supervision and leadership of Dr. Yombo Awojobi of the Awojobi Clinic, Eruwa on 24th March, 2010. The clinic has a qualified Doctor on call, and it is used by the Osun State Medical Students Association (OSUNMSA) of the College of Medicine, University of Ibadan/ University College Hospital, Ibadan, and the Medical Students Association of the Obafemi Awolowo University/Obafemi Awolowo Teaching Hospital Complex, for their respective annual medical retreats. In addition, the former Association also provides routine medical screening on a quarterly basis, at Orile-Isotun. Courtesy of sponsors, medicines and surgical procedures are provided free during the retreats. Also, surgical procedures when they are not sponsored, are guaranteed to be affordable.

In view of the ineffectiveness of the Government to ensure regular and prompt attendance of school by teachers on the grounds that the student population does not warrant such attention, the community built and registered its own nursery and primary school. Thus, unlike the policy-makers of Osun State, we believe that even if only one student is available and willing to attend school, provision should be made for him to do so. Enrollment in Isotun is forty-five (45) and in Orile-Isotun thirty-six (36). The school provides free education and one free meal a day. It has been providing the free meal long before the State Government adopted it. The school building is conducive and there is one teacher to each class. We recently introduced computer education. In November 2018, the land donated by Isotun and two other communities at Orile-Isotun, was handed by the Executive Governor of the state, to the Deeper Life Christian Ministry for the establishment of a University—The Deeper Life University, Orilemeta, Ilesa.

We tapped into the rural electrification programme of the Federal Government to provide electricity supply to three (3) settlements at Isotun and its environment, and to eleven (11) settlements in Orile-Isotun. The church has been rebuilt to befit its status of the National Headquarters of The Most Glorious Apostolic Church Divine Atundaolu.

CHAPTER 11

PARADISE LOST AND PARADISE REGAINED

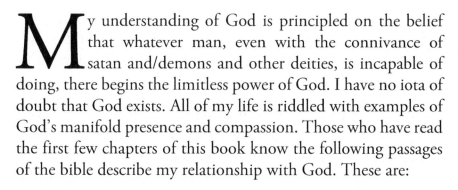

My understanding of God is principled on the belief that whatever man, even with the connivance of satan and/demons and other deities, is incapable of doing, there begins the limitless power of God. I have no iota of doubt that God exists. All of my life is riddled with examples of God's manifold presence and compassion. Those who have read the first few chapters of this book know the following passages of the bible describe my relationship with God. These are:

a) *Psalm 23 verses 4 and 5:*

1. *Yea, though I walk through the valley of the shadow of death I will fear no evil: for thou art with me; thy rod and thy staff they comfort me.*

2. *Thou preparest a table before me in the presence of my enemies: thou anointest my head with oil; my cup runneth over; and*

b) *Psalm 91 verse 13: Thou shalt tread upon the lion and adder: the young lion and the dragon shalt thou trample under thy feet.*

Even though my mother had a Muslim background, I knew her, even in my childhood, to be a Christian. I was, therefore, born into a Christian home and I know my parents to have initially been Anglicans. They attended St. Peter's Anglican Church, Bukuru near Jos and I attended St. Peter's Anglican Primary School, Bukuru. My father was a Lay Reader, and before I was even ten years old, I was a member of the choir.

On the relocation of the family to Lagos, we switched to the Baptist denomination and all the children of school-going-age attended Surulere Baptist School, then located on Ojuelegba Road. At the Baptist Academy I headed, in my fourth year, the Baptist Training Union which is now called the Baptist Students' Fellowship. While in the boarding house at the Baptist Academy, we (students) attended Somolu Baptist Church where I was also a Sunday school teacher. Even though I had been baptized in the Anglican Church in 1951, it was not by immersion so, I had to repeat baptism in the First Baptist Church, Broad Street, Lagos where my grandfather had been baptized some sixty-three years earlier.

In June 2018, I was awarded the honour of being A Life Patron of the Youth Fellowship at First Baptist Church in Aipate, Iwo. Also, in 2019, I was nominated and elected the Chairman of the Board of Trustees of my church, Bodija Estate Baptist Church, Old Bodija, Ibadan.

In the summer of 1966, the year I arrived in the United States, I decided against the wish/advice of my sponsors to visit Watts, in Los Angeles, to satisfy my curiosity about its deplorable state which was the reason for the 1964 riot by blacks and which I had read about in some United States magazines --Newsweek and Time--while I was in Nigeria. I travelled in the company of Mohammed Elmi, a foreign student from Somalia. The experience was so horrible that it left a twenty-year indelible mark on my mind. I had never, ever seen, in my life, the squalor that was Watts. We stayed overnight in a dingy hotel.

After this visit, I started wondering whether there was one God for the whites and another for the blacks. It was unimaginable to me that the same God would be so kind to one race and so much more less compassionate to another. This was at the heart of the religious crisis which I went through in the next twenty years. In the mist of the crisis, I remember that I had read in Winston Churchill's "My Early Life" that most children from good Christian backgrounds would in their adult life, go through a religious crisis. He described his own experience and the several futile and endless inquiry he and his friends in the military made on the subject matter. In the end, they agreed that what was paramount was "Healthy Mindedness." In my own case, I read several books on religion beginning with "Being and Nothingness" by Jean-Paul Sartre. Of all the religious books I read, this book made the most profound impact on my religious life. I became an Agnostic where I could easily have been an Atheist. For the next twenty years I did not attend church services except on special and inevitable occasions of marriage/funeral of close friends or relatives.

On 4th August, 1986, as I was returning home to Nigeria at the end of my engagement by the United Nations, I carefully reviewed not only my tour of duty in Dakar, Senegal, but also my entire life. It was a life full of favour and mercy from "Some Being". It could not have been an accident: my association with Hal Sheller, my schooling at California State and at Claremont e.t.c. So, who was this Being that took so much interest in my affairs? After a long period of examination on the plane, and a brief review of Bolaji E. Idowu's concept of destiny in Yoruba mythology as espoused in his book " Olodumare: God in Yoruba Belief", I concluded that the Almighty God was that "Being." Now that I had arrived at this inevitable conclusion, what was I to do?

117

I resolved that, on arriving home that night in Ibadan, I would kneel down and thank Him for being so gracious to me, even in moments of neglect of his benevolence. However, how was I to say the prayer in a house and before wife and children who for twenty years had not seen me pray? They would think, if they caught me praying, that there was some calamity or catalogue of catastrophes I was desperate to ward off. In view of this, I decided the thank offering would be done after everyone had gone to sleep. So, that night, when everyone had gone to sleep, I rose up from my bed and in my prayer, I reviewed how God had been very kind to me in spite of my idiosyncrasies and I thanked him. I told him I had not come to ask for ANYTHING but to simply thank Him. I returned to the faith and continued from where I had left off.

Two years later, I was a nominee for the stool of the Asotun of Isotun and not a few people thought that I should banish the idea because of the danger it posed to my faith. I knew I would face a number of challenges about my faith but I thought I had made up my mind to be a Christian. I wondered till this day about leaders of our faith who discourage us from being politicians or traditional rulers. If we abandon these professions, then faithfuls of other religions would dominate them to our detriment. There have been several instances when those I invited to be Chiefs have been persuaded not to accept my invitation for reason of faith. So, if all kingmakers, traditional chiefs and courtiers are non-Christians, when and how will the institution of Obaship change for the good of Christendom? Even today, few people believe that I am a genuine Christian, but I am not perturbed. They will find out in heaven that I will receive acclaim and admission before many who on earth assume very high degree of piety. Of course, I have received invitations to be anything else but a Christian but I have never accepted the invitation and by the grace of God, I will continue to repose all of my faith in God the Father, the Son, and the Holy Ghost.

I am a member of the Association of Born Again Christian Obas of Osun State and I have the special spiritual gift of healing, and of dreams. I am also privileged to have God speak to me directly on selected issues. May the will of God in my life be done!

Religion

As Member Of The Choir At St Peters Anglican Church
Bukuru, Jos

Baptist Students Fellowship At Comprehensive High
School Aiyetoro

CHAPTER 12

FAMILY

My childhood friend, Iyabo Gladys Knox-Rollings, and I were married at The First Methodist Church, Fullerton, California, United States of America on 12th September, 1969. There were a total of 250 guests hosted by the Shellers. My wife is of Sierra Leonian extraction. Her father, Osie Hamilton Rollings, was with the Customs and Excise in the colonial era and was posted at varying times to Calabar, Warri and Lagos. He retired in 1951 but was again engaged on contract till his demise on 10th April, 1962. Her mother, Gladys Millicent Knox-Rollings, was a trained nurse and midwife who worked as a Volunteer Officer of the Red Cross Society of Nigeria at the Spastic Clinic, Royal Orthopedic Hospital, Igbobi, Lagos. She was later employed as a full-time Care Giver at the same clinic in 1957 and traces her roots to Igbore, Abeokuta, Ogun State, Nigeria.

My wife was the last of five children and the only one by her mother. She intimated to me while we were courting that her preferred profession was in the hospital setting. In realizing this ambition, she was engaged at the Ahmadu Bello University Institute of Health as Administrative Officer II in 1974 and later as Administrative Officer II at the 900-bed University College

Hospital, Ibadan in 1975. She rose at this latter institution to the peak of her professional career as Director of Administration. Both parents bequeathed to her landed property in Lagos.

The family is blessed with three children and three grandchildren. Akintunde who was our first child, was born on 30th May, 1970. Two years after his birth we noticed that his eyes were frequently jaundiced. We were referred to the Children's Hospital in Los Angeles where after investigation we were informed that he was a sickle cell disease carrier and would have an average age of no more than 16-19 years, given the state of medical advancement at the time. The bad news had a number of implications. It meant that the genotype for my wife and I was AS and that each pregnancy would have a twenty-five percent probability of producing a sickler.

Our son, Akintunde, attended the University of Ibadan Staff School but did not gain admission into the International School, University of Ibadan. Deliberate efforts were made by many friends especially Professor Yemi Onibokun (nee Apantaku) to extract some concession from the management of the school, without luck. We opted for Abadina College and arranged for him to go to a good school in Britain in the summer to make up for any deficiencies. During my sabbatical leave in 1984, we visited Hal Sheller and his family in Springfield, Oregon, in the United States of America during which the Sheller family requested that we allow one of our three children come to stay with them. Since the request was made just before our departure from Springfield, Oregon, we agreed to consider it and revert to them. The choice was between Akintunde who was fourteen (14) and Morounmubo who was ten (10). Even though the obvious preference by the Shellers was for the latter because, as I surmised, the Shellers had three boys and Morounmubo would have been good company for Gayle. However, given my experience, she was too young for such an adventure and besides, being the first female, she was very much attached to her mother. We therefore decided on Akintunde who after his summer school in Britain in 1985, proceeded on to Springfield High School, Oregon, as an exchange student. In taking this decision I was to clear from him whether he was comfortable with two things: making a switch to Springfield in the academic year in which he was to graduate, and the fact that in the USA. he would not graduate from high school until he was eighteen. His answers were in the affirmative. Indeed, he confided in me that "I will learn a lot".

In view of the military coup of 1985 in Nigeria, I was not able to join him in London for the trip to the USA. I joined him in Springfield a week later and had a meeting with the school counsellor. I was privileged to be given a tour of the school's facilities: the metal works and woodwork workshops to mention a few. I also attended some of his classes with him. These included the history and the biology classes. I was very impressed and happy that Akintunde was going to have the best educational training ever. The biology class was exceptional; it was a miniature zoo. The teacher started the lesson by bringing out a live snake from its cage and feeding it with a rat. What a quality standard of education.

As I took a walk to the dentist after this visit, two things crossed my mind: first, I wished I was young again and had this same opportunity; second, I wondered how it was possible for Nigerian Students like me who had graduated from Nigerian schools to cope so well and to excel in the universities in this environment. As it turned out, we did not have to spend much on Akintunde. The Shellers paid for his mid-day meal in the years he spent in the high school and he won several scholarships for his tuition at University of Oregon, Eugene, Oregon, where he obtained his first degree in Economics and a Master's Degree in Urban and Regional Planning.

We arranged and paid for him to visit home annually in Nigeria through 1992. He married Seun Adeoye on 1st November, 2003, and the marriage was blessed with a male child, Akinkunmi Owosekun. My wife and I named him Adeyemi. He had several health challenges and the Sheller family with whom he lived till he was eighteen--his graduation from high school--provided the much-needed support. In 1990, he fell grievously ill and it looked very much like the demise which the Los Angeles Children's Hospital had predicted was imminent. He was hospitalized for weeks and there were many anxious moments of waiting. Miraculously, he survived it but had run up a bill of over $30,000.00. NISER under Prof. Dotun Phillips was so sympathetic that it provided assistance of $7,000.00. He lived some twenty-one years thereafter but succumbed to recurring bouts of brain cancer on 5th January, 2012, some four months short of his 42nd birthday.

I have provided such details of Akintunde's health history largely because in Yoruba culture/mythology, especially the occultic world, it is generally believed that the highly successful in the traditional setting do so by sacrificing their first male child. Well, we did no such thing and we advise those who may be contemplating it to banish the idea.

Morounmubo was born in Zaria, in 1974. She attended University of Ibadan Staff Primary School and St. Louis Grammar School, Mokola, Ibadan. She obtained her first degree in Political Science at the University of Ibadan in 1997 followed by an MSc degree in International Relations (1999) from the same University. In 2001, she obtained an MBA degree in Information Technology from the private Christian University of La Verne, La Verne, California, USA. She was for seventeen years an Annuity Analyst and later a Compliance

Manager at the American International Group (AIG) which is ranked as one of the foremost insurance companies in the world. She is married to Oluwafemi A. Bolaji of Okelele, Ilorin, Kwara State, and the marriage is blessed with two boys.

Our second daughter, Jolaade, was born in Ibadan in 1977. She attended the University of Ibadan Staff School and International School. In 2001, she obtained her first degree in Law, also from University of Ibadan. She followed in her sister's footsteps and obtained an MBA from the University of La Verne, California, in 2003. Her concentration was in Finance. She was admitted to the New York and California Bar in 2009 and 2013, respectively. She has worked in various capacities as a lawyer, engaging in Public Interest Law. For almost ten years, she ran her own private practice on Wilshire Blvd., in Los Angeles. For several years, she protected the rights of parents in the child welfare system. She continues to protect the interests of the public in her current role as a government attorney. Like her parents, she has always given back to her community, engaging in pro bono work in and around the Los Angeles, California area.

Family

With Olori

With Children

With Siblings

With Hal Sheller

With Akintunde And Akinkunmi

Morounmubo And Grandma
Mary Sheller

Grandpa Harry Lynn Sheller
with Morounmubo (L) And
Akintunde

Olori And I With 'Femi, Morounmubo And Their Children

Olori And I With Morounmubo And Jolaade

CHAPTER 13

THE EVENTIDE

A few years from my retirement from NISER, two of my bosom friends, Surveyor Lawrence Layi Arinola and Professor Ode Ojowu, and I indulged in the estimation of the level of income which would be required to sustain our respective pre-retirement standard of living. The estimates were troubling. They were indicative of the fact that the resources I would require after retirement to maintain my pre-retirement standard of living would be much bigger than the resources which were at my disposal in my service years. I therefore prayed specially to God to take due cognizance of this possible reality and to make available to me, in my retirement, a lot more resources than he did during my service years.

\In April, 2002 one year ahead of my retirement from NISER, I registered a Limited Liability Consultancy company with the Corporate Affairs Commission (CAC), and in 2006 I was awarded a contract under the World Bank Economic Reform and Government Project (ERGP CREDIT NO 4011-UNI) to train staff of the newly established National Bureau of Statistics (NBS) in the elaboration and use of both the macro-econometric and the input-output models of the Nigerian economy. This contract was most rewarding both professionally and financially. Also, in the period 2015 to 2017, I used the same consulting company to source for consultants for a number of training workshops in the National Planning Commission. These workshops were financed under the Support to Federal Government Reform Programme (SUFEGOR) of the European Union. However, the most rewarding and intriguing of the engagements were yet to come.

In mid-2019, I received a call from one of my junior colleagues who had been my Research Assistant in virtually every Ministry, Department or Agency (MDA) in which I had served. He intimated to me that he had just been elevated to the position of Director of Macroeconomic Analysis in the Federal Ministry of Finance Budget and National Planning and confided in me that he was desirous of leaving a legacy in two areas which he itemized as follow:

a) *The elaboration of a portfolio of models which would be domiciled in the Department. He explained that in spite of the general belief that the department relied heavily on the use of quantitative tools in planning, policy formulation and policy analysis, there was not, in fact, any such quantitative tool in the Ministry. He intimated that the situation was desperate because Government was already looking up to his department to deliver on both a medium-term plan 2021-2025 and a long-term perspective plan 2026-2050; and*

b) *Capacity building within the Department in the elaboration, use and operationalization of the models.*

The new Director, Mr. David Taiwo Adeosun, requested to know if I would be willing to provide some assistance to him in this Herculean Task. In considering this request, I gave some thought to the current criminalization of old age in our social, political and academic life and to what detractors might make of my involvement. However, I was also flattered. All things considered, I obliged the Director.

In the month of November of the same year I received a phone call from the Director informing me that he had obtained the Honourable Minister's approval for a one-week training for twenty (20) members of his staff, in the elaboration of macro-econometric model and input-output analysis, and that he would want me to organize the training programme which was scheduled to take place in the first half of November. I quickly put together a team comprising very experienced professionals. These included my longtime associate and colleague, Professor Vincent O. Akinyosoye, with whom I had been working on the macro-econometric model since 1982. He had risen to become the First Statistician General of the Federation (retired); Professor Victor O. Okoruwa, of the Department of Agricultural Economics and current Director of Academic Planning, University of Ibadan, and Professor Babatunde W. Adeoye of the Department of Economics, University of Lagos with whom I had updated the NISER macro-econometric model in 2007.

Two weeks after the training programme, we were requested by the Ministry to prepare, using models that were already at our disposal, a report on the bottlenecks of the Nigeria Economy, which bottlenecks would if eliminated, facilitate higher growth of all other sectors of the economy and culminate in much higher GDP growth rate and employment generation while lowering the rate of inflation. This report was duly completed and submitted in December, 2019.

In early 2020, we were invited to a retreat that was organized by the ministry and scheduled for the last week of February, to deliberate on the appropriate models for the elaboration of the proposed medium-term plan 2021-2025 and long-term plan 2026-2050. At the retreat, I showcased the macro-econometric model which I had used successfully to advise Mr. President while I headed IPG, and a recently elaborated input-output table for 2018. There were no comparable long-term models to consider at the retreat. Our outing was most successful. The retreat resolved that updated versions of the macro-econometric model and input-output tables be commissioned for the medium-term plan while a Computable General Equilibrium model be commissioned for the long-term perspective plan.

In April 2020, the Ministry advertised in national newspapers for a broad range of services required for the preparation of the medium-term plan. We applied and won the bids for both the econometric and input-output models. We elaborated a macro-econometric model of about 300 equations and dynamic input-output tables (2020-2026) for a time period long enough to generate an investment plan for the medium-term plan. Our contributions to the planning effort are the following:

a) *Identification of the bottlenecks of the Nigerian economy through 2025;*

b) *Demonstration that the application of resources to the bottlenecks alone leads to a higher improvement in social welfare than the simultaneous application of plan resources to all sectors of the economy;*

c) *If plan resources are applied only to the bottleneck sectors the economy would grow at double digit rate beginning form 2026;*

d) *If (b) and (c) are adopted the resource requirement of the medium-term plan will be far less (about 56 percent) of what was envisioned.*

The models were subsequently used to train the planners and was validated at a retreat to which all economic ministries, the Central Bank of Nigeria, the Presidential Advisory Committee, and all development partners were invited. Additionally, the models are today domiciled in the ministry's laboratory. This laboratory was commissioned in 2022 at an elaborate ceremony attended by the development partners. We were most grateful to God, the Honourable Minister, and the Director Macroeconomic Analysis for the opportunity to play a major role in the formulation of the medium-term plan. Note, however, that it is not over until it is all over!

In early 2022, there were reported hitches with the preparation of the long-term perspective plan compelling the Ministry to re-advertise for consultancy services for the appropriate model and the Macroeconomic framework for the perspective plan. I was somewhat reluctant to take up this assignment largely because the Dynamic Computable General Equilirium model required was not my cup of tea. I made enquiries and it was clear to me that my company was the preferred candidate. However, I was not going to be persuaded to take on the assignment unless I could get on board, the most reputable consultant in Dynamic Computable Gerneral Equilibrium model in the person of Dr. Alarudeen Aminu who was the Acting Director of the Centre for Econometrics and Allied Research (CEAR) at the Department of Economics, University of Ibadan. I was also concerned that he could easily have been engaged by a competitor. My team was lucky that he was available and willing to work under my leadership. But there was still one major constraint. A Dynamic CGE model could not be built in less than six (6) months but the Ministry had a luxury of only two (2) months. We assessed the situation against the background of the fact that we already had elaborated the required input-output table which is the foundation for the Dynamic CGE model. Having hedged against the manpower and time constraints we decided to take up the challenge.

We were awarded the contract on the 28th of February, 2022, with a brief which included the following:

a) *Take as given, the United Nations estimated population of Nigeria of 411 million by 2050;*

133

b) *Elaborate a model and design a Macroeconomic framework that would propel the Nigerian economy to generate double digit Gross Domestic Product (GDP) growth rate consistently for a period of ten (10) to fifteen (15) years;*

c) *Raise the per capita income in Nigeria to over $12,000 by 2050 such that Nigeria becomes a member of the elite club of the Upper-Middle Income Developing countries by 2050;*

d) *Generate high level of employment that would reduce the incidence of poverty to less than ten (10) million people by 2050.*

This assignment was completed within four months. However, " the jury is still out " on what contribution this report will make to the development of our country, going forward.

Who would have thought that these contributions to knowledge and the development effort reported in this chapter would be realizable in the twilight of my mortality.

OWOSEKUN RULING HOUSE FAMILY TREE

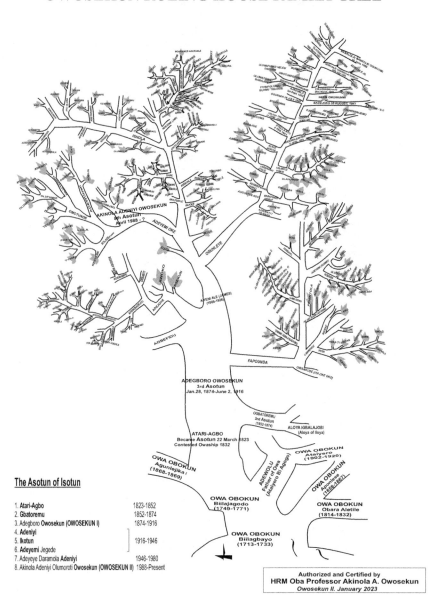

The Asotun of Isotun

1. Atari-Agbo — 1823-1852
2. Gbatoremu — 1852-1874
3. Adegboro **Owosekun** (OWOSEKUN I) — 1874-1916
4. Adeniyi
5. **Ikotun** — 1916-1946
6. Adeyemi Jegede
7. Adeyeye Daramola **Adeniyi** — 1946-1980
8. Akinola Adeniyi Olumoroti **Owosekun** (OWOSEKUN II) — 1988-Present

Authorized and Certified by
HRM Oba Professor Akinola A. Owosekun
Owosekun II. January 2023

135

SUBERU OLALEYE FAMILY TREE

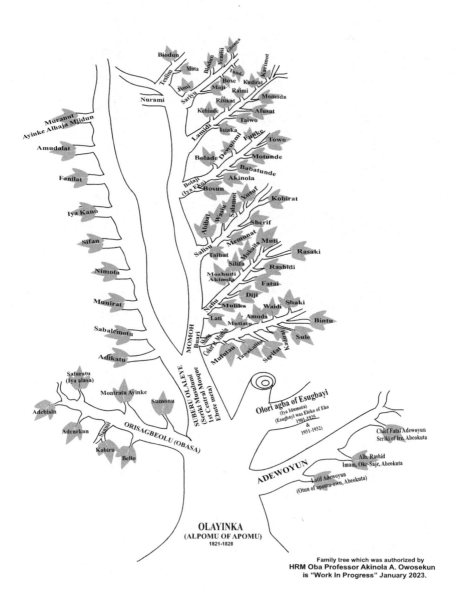

Family tree which was authorized by
**HRM Oba Professor Akinola A. Owosekun
is "Work In Progress" January 2023.**